Naimah and Ajmal
On Newton's Mountain

a novella by

Nancy Dafoe

Finishing Line Press
Georgetown, Kentucky

Naimah and Ajmal
On Newton's Mountain

Copyright © 2021 by Nancy Dafoe
ISBN 978-1-64662-537-6 First Edition
All rights reserved under International and Pan-American Copyright Conventions.
No part of this book may be reproduced in any manner whatsoever without written permission from the publisher, except in the case of brief quotations embodied in critical articles and reviews.

ACKNOWLEDGMENTS

The author would like to gratefully acknowledge Finishing Line Press' Leah Maines, Kevin Maines, and Christen Kincaid for publishing her novella and books of poetry. She would also like to thank her former students who inspired her and told of their sadness, their experiences as immigrants, and their fears during wars. She would like to thank her former student, the immensely talented Katie Mulligan who created the cover image of Naimah for this contemporary fable/novella.

Publisher: Leah Huete de Maines
Editor: Christen Kincaid
Cover Art: Katie Mulligan, Scholastic Gold Portfolio Winner, former student of the author's, and current professional illustrator, used with artist's permission
Author Photo: Parker Stone
Cover Design: Elizabeth Maines McCleavy

Order online: www.finishinglinepress.com
also available on amazon.com

Author inquiries and mail orders:
Finishing Line Press
P. O. Box 1626
Georgetown, Kentucky 40324
U. S. A.

Table of Contents

I. Sleeping Infant Missing 1

II. Ahura Mazda Protector 7

III. No Sign of Ajmal 13

IV. Makram and Language Below Language 19

V. Naimah Welcomed by Widows 25

VI. Baltasar and Ajmal Roam Perterra 31

VII. Another Dangerous Man 37

VIII. Ajmal Discovers Man's Violence 43

IX. Naimah Writes 51

X. Viper Faraj Instructs 57

XI. Naimah Speaks About Peace 65

XII. Edge of Perterra 73

XIII. Naimah Considers Newton's Mountain 79

XIV. Leaving Perterra 85

XV. Marketing, Branding, and the Selling of a Promise 91

XVI. Ajmal Finds a Brother 95

XVII. Unfamiliar Familiar 101

*Dedicated to my beautiful son
Blaise Martin Dafoe (1987-2019)*

*and to refugee mothers and children
separated from one another worldwide.*

I

Sleeping Infant Missing

Scurrying over broken mud bricks and plaster, a wall lizard approached the baby's head. Dotted in black ink splats covering its light green skin, this six-inch reptile looked quite ordinary to any who might have been awake in the night holding a flashlight. The lizard had somehow managed to survive in a kill zone in disputed territory in the Middle East.

Although wall lizards are quadrupedal and typically move rapidly, using their four limbs and tail, this one stopped cold near the sleeping baby Ajmal. Narrowing its lizard eyes, Akeem, the wise, studied the boy as if to speak, then stretched out with its front claws. In the instant the lizard made the most delicate contact near the blue birthmark at the corner of the baby's left eye, Ajmal stirred and flapped his arms, kicking his legs rapidly.

"Wake up," the lizard whispered in a voice too quiet for most human ears. "Run, run now. You must wake and run," Akeem exhorted.

Ajmal instantly opened his large eyes and began crying with urgency, sending a shiver through his dreaming aunt.

"What's happening?" the baby's aunt Tabani, whose name meant bright like moonlight, woke. She sat up on her mattress that was thrown on a bare floor. "Oh, no. Get up! Quickly, quickly!" the boy's aunt yelled, brought to consciousness by the child's yell first then by the noise of distant bombs exploding, unaware of the speaking lizard. "Naimah, come at once." Tabani pulled on her sister's arm.

"What is it?" Naimah said, startled. "What is wrong, my sister?" Naimah heard the sounds of war come to them and grabbed Ajmal, curling him to her chest.

"We must go. They are nearly upon us," Tabani warned.

Before Naimah fled, she clutched only her hijab and a thin blanket for the baby, swaddling him as she awkwardly but quickly climbed over and around rubble and the sheltering space that had been their temporary home.

Tabani tripped and started to fall but caught herself by pushing her hand against a partially collapsed wall. Dust and dirt dove into the small cut across her palm. Never yelling in pain, she set her foot and moved on, knowing they must leave the crippled buildings.

*

Naimah scrambled down a dirt road, her sister not far behind. Looking down to avoid pock marks in the road, she felt her breathing too rapidly.

Detonation of a bomb shuddered through her, causing her an involuntarily spasm. Bursting shrapnel split the air with black metal rushing everywhere. Loud voices penetrated, coming nearer. Young mother gripped her infant more tightly. Bullets whizzed past like swarms of angry bees of death.

Barefoot and in night clothing, the sisters ran, scarcely speaking for several moments. Darkness punctuated only with bursts of startling light flashes. On a narrow, dusty road, partially riven, sisters recited prayers wordlessly before Tabani broke their silent pact.

"Why?" yelled Tabani. "Why are they shooting at us? You have a child. We are nothing to them."

Naimah looked back at her younger sister, wishing the girl was faster on her feet. "Ehh." Many thoughts ran through Naimah's head in response to her sister's demanding questions, but she could not seem to form whole words. "Yulp." Only a garbled sound came out which did not register with Tabani who felt as if her feet dragged weights behind them. All her quickness of youth fell away in fear.

Concentrating on her heart beating to the rapid rhythm of her feet, Naimah could almost hear her husband Nabil urge her to go faster, *"chegil, chegil."* He had been gone over a year, killed in another town, but Naimah still felt his presence often, encouraging her to continue. Nabil was with her for that moment before disappearing again. Even his ghost could not hold out against such onslaught.

"Alllleee"

As the older sister Naimah bolted with her infant son wrapped in her arms, she looked back toward the shriek. More than all the gunfire, this high-pitched sound ruptured Naimah's ears and she stopped. "Noooo," she cried out. Her little sister Tabani had fallen.

Naimah turned and moved quickly toward the tangled heap that her sister had become. Rapid shocks of staccato gunfire burst around Naimah, spitting earth in multiple directions. Tabani's once beautiful mouth hung open in gapping dark hole, her eyes too wide. The girl's legs had been tossed over her head at an impossible angle with bone exposed to wind and noxious smells of smoke and death. Leaning over and reaching her free hand down to cover Tabani's eyes, Naimah swallowed too hard, hurting her throat. Then she was standing again, in motion before stumbling, screams attempting to rise. She was in full flight away from guns, away even from her little sister. "Not Tabani. No, not Tabani," Naimah whispered as she then heard only her son's vital breath.

*

The sleeping baby boy Ajmal could feel his mother's heart. His hair was black as a cloudless night, his lips full, his breath sweet, Naimah had told everyone. His bright, dark eyes were graced with long lashes. Ajmal rode undisturbed by the jostle of his mother's rapid, jerking movements. In his mother's arms, he knew no better place.

"I will not let anything happen to you, my beautiful boy," Naimah said to Ajmal as she zig-zagged down the road, trying to dodge shrapnel. "No harm will come to you, I promise. I will save you."

Blinding flashes again. Indiscriminate pain hit and burst through Naimah. Complete eclipse fell like stone.

*

Ajmal flew from Naimah's arms. Startled, not frightened, he caught and held his breath as he traveled through air. He only found his voice when landing with a plop in a pool of soft, muddy earth and rain water. Chill of the water and earth prompted his rapid, gasping breaths. Ajmal's cries instantly rose to faint screams before his protector landed.

*

Soldiers carrying heavy assault weapons marched past Naimah, glancing down at her. One young soldier broke his column, stopped, nudged the woman's body with the toe of his boot to be sure, before shaking his head and fitting back into an irregular line. Faces hardened, beards bushy, the soldiers were covered in black smudges and dirt. They wore no remorse, but a few still wore the blood of their fallen comrades. A command. Suddenly quiet, the men stopped and listened. They heard nothing more but the sounds of their own breathing. They were instructed to continue than warily. Guns lowered at last, they picked up their heads, craning their necks to see if anything moved up ahead.

II

Ahura Mazda Protector

Plop. Ajmal's whimpers went unheeded until a frog hopped on him. Like all frogs, the one landing on the baby's forehead had bulging eyes and smooth, slimy skin. It certainly did not look intelligent or capable of helping an infant when a rush of air passed through its inflated vocal pouch at the bottom of its mouth. CROOOAK! Ajmal stopped crying at the frog's voice and slippery touch.

Ahura Mazda pushed air past his vocal sac again, the second time out of delight with his own song. Fortunately for Ajmal, Ahura Mazda knew what to do when a human baby appeared out of nowhere and landed in his domain. In the baby's extraordinary flight, flung from his injured mother's arms, he had crossed over into Perterra.

"GOOROK. Welcome, boy," he said. "Looks like I'll be busy with you for some time, little one."

It was as if Ahura Mazda's entire existence had been intended for this moment: how to feed the infant Ajmal, how to protect the babe from drowning. Again, Ahura Mazda's knowledge was good luck for Ajmal. But babies have many more needs than just to be saved from drowning and hunger.

Ajmal stirred, kicked his little legs, feeling the weight of the frog. With parachute-like webbing, Ahura Mazda spread a wide foot across Ajmal's forehead and nearly over one of the baby's eyes. Ajmal blinked twice. Webbed foot remained. The frog noticed the baby's little blue birthmark under the muddy covering.

Releasing a foamy mass, frogspawn to be exact, around the baby, Ahura Mazda pushed the baby along. Wiggling tadpoles ready to hatch out of their egg sacs moved in multiple directions slightly, gently messaging the baby's skin. Continued motion of these immature amphibians also warmed Ajmal.

Ahura Mazda spoke to the infant in low, soothing tones that sounded rather like a bullfrog to the untrained or unintended ear. Although his voice was a little froggy, Ahura Mazda could speak multiple languages, and even the unspoken communication that existed below verbal utterance. All this is what Ajmal heard and felt as his plump body slid down an embankment.

As Ajmal smiled for the first time in days, Ahura Mazda released an air bubble around the baby's face, allowing Ajmal to breathe freely in water. "You're about to take a journey," said Ahura Mazda. "And you'll need to be comfortable under water, something you humans have never perfected."

"Now, as to how you got here and what this all means, you'll have to wait until you're older for those stories. For now, let's just focus on developing your curiosity, managing your eating and drinking, identifying the voices of other creatures you hear, and our watery journey."

Inside an air bubble, a thin secretion of milky liquid found its way to the baby's lips. Ajmal drank hungrily and fell asleep again, dreaming of his mother's softness, her voice. He was still listening to her heartbeat. At his young age, just being held close by his mother was a kind of nourishment. In this drowsy state, he drank as if he could never have enough.

"You're a hungry one. Ah, but your good fortune is you landed right next to me," said Ahura Mazda. "My good luck is you're quiet for a human. You have no idea how hard it is to care for a constantly crying baby." Ahura Mazda said this as if he was well experienced in such difficulties and expected some level of appreciation from Ajmal who would give him none.

*

"I once existed in the realm of men," Ahura Mazda said as they floated along, "to answer the question you have not yet asked. As you will one day know, I saw not a drop of harmony in that kingdom where hatreds are generational and spill over from men to animals. Amphibians, too. Yes, man's anger affects all living creatures in your world."

Ajmal squirmed for a few moments before burping loudly. The burp floated around the bubble.

"Well, that was a good one. You should be more comfortable now," Ahura Mazda continued. "Long ago, I crossed into Perterra with only occasional forays back into that other domain where even Earth bears the scars of man's violence. One of those scars was carved into rock at the side of the now pock-marked road where your mother lay unconscious and bleeding. I can anticipate your questions even if you can't form them yet, so don't judge me too harshly. If I could have taken her, too, I would have, but you see, it's not up to me. She was unable to cross over."

Ahura Mazda croaked again loudly. GROOOCK. "I guess I will be more comfortable, too. You will learn the fate of your mother one day, but my concern is to help you survive your first year. Admittedly, you won't remember any of this, but it's still important that I tell you what I know. Something I say may slip into your unconscious mind and remain."

Ajmal smiled again, listening to the croaking frog as they moved through the water like fish. The tadpole eggs surrounded them both completely.

Because it was November when the hot, dry climate submits to humidity in Perterra, as well as in man's Middle Eastern countries, it began raining again. Little Ajmal was pulled more quickly by swirling, small currents. The babe floated with the frog as his guide and protector. "You will be quite a challenge, I'm afraid," said Ahura Mazda to Ajmal. "If I keep you alive, I will have done a fine job. It has been some time since I raised a human as young as you." Here, Ahura Mazda was greatly exaggerating since it was a long time before that he had even ventured into the realm of men and then only to leap out of the way of stomping feet. He listened attentively to their loud voices, to the shattering of rocks and lives before gratefully returning to Perterra.

"As you can imagine, Perterra suits me much better," he said. "I think it will suit you, too."

Together, the little troupe of frog, baby, and developing tadpoles in their egg mass were swept along for miles deeper into Perterra, leaving far behind violent men and a warring world.

Within this foamy mass, Ajmal was comforted and listened to Ahura Mazda's voice tell him fabulous stories that meant nothing but sounded lovely.

"I blew my throat twice as big as my body and let out a loud belch that frightened the monster away, and that human child rode the currents with me all the way to our ninth sea. He was much bigger than you when he accidentally landed. You can imagine the surprise on both our faces when he sat up beside me. Here I was minding my own business when a human child flies down almost on top of me. If I wasn't so quick, that boy might have squished me. His first word was 'Mama.' Then he said, 'Froggie,' and he thought it was funny. We were like a comedy team with me having all the straight lines."

Ajmal did not understand anything the talkative Ahura Mazda said, but the narratives flowed over him and began to work in mysterious ways to help him form language and relationships. Big bulging eyes of the frog were kind and intelligent, staring into the curious, needy, narrowed eyes of the baby.

"You are unimportant now, little one," croaked Ahura Mazda, "but one day, you will be essential apparently. Anyone can make a difference, no matter how small the act or gesture." Ahura Mazda might have said this of himself, but he was speaking of and to the human child again. They dropped into deeper clear water as the rivulet moved over rocks and into a pool.

Little Ajmal struggled momentarily in the water as Ahura Mazda spoke. "You see, you don't have to be big to assist others. I was once as insignificant as you are at this moment. I had no idea what I was capable of doing when I was a mere tadpole. Just move your arms and legs. That's it."

Ajmal began swimming with the frog still on his head, feeling all the world wet but not frightening. Tadpoles squirmed and wiggled beside him, tickling the baby.

III

No Sign of Ajmal

Raafe wrapped a cloth, torn from another man's shirt, around a wounded man's arm, taking care not to pull too tightly. "OOH," the old man groaned.

"They shoot old men and women and children," said Raafe angrily. One of the medics came over to him, checking the wound and the crude dressing.

"Thank you. I can take it from here," said medic Tariq. "You've been up all night, I know."

"It's the least I—" Raafe's voice trailed off, looking around the space crammed with cots and wounded. "I'm looking for my cousins," he said, eyes imploring.

Tariq pursed his lips tightly. "No one. Not from your descriptions. There are a few little ones, but, as you know, none of them matched the child—"

"Ajmal, Naimah's beautiful baby."

"I'm sorry. We can handle this now. Go. Go find your cousins. They may be safe yet."

"There is nowhere safe."

*

Raafe tried not to drag his tired feet as he clambered over and around rubble in the city to his mother's house. Wrapping their arms around one another, Raafe kissed the top of her graying head. "Al-am, any word yet from Tabani or Naimah?"

"Nothing, my boy," Jumana sighed. "You must find them, but first something to eat."

"No," said Raafe. "I will eat after I find them. He took a drink from the cup his mother put in his hands then left again. Jumana stood at the open window, nervously wiping the frame with a cloth.

"Come back to me, my son."

*

Raafe spotted Naimah's sister Tabani first, sprinting to her broken heap of a body. "No!" He yelled before falling to his knees and weeping. In despair, the tall, thin young man held Tabani's head in his hands, stroked her long dark hair. "It's not possible," he repeated. He almost did not recognize his cousin's once beautiful face, frozen in distortion of death. Then he thought of Naimah.

Scrambling to his feet, he realized that the sister must be nearby. Further up the road, Raafe detected a shape, near a drainage ditch. He caught his breath then let out a cry. Naimah was flat on her back. Raafe bent down and touched her cheek. His heart nearly stopped. She was breathing. Whispering a small prayer of thanks, Raafe put his hands under her head and shoulders, the living sister who needed medical attention and could still be saved. The gash on her head was still slowly bleeding but the blood had already started to congeal.

"Alive," said Raafe to himself but out loud. "Where is your son?" Raafe took off his jacket and placed it under Naimah's head then jumped up and looked in the very ditch into which the baby had flown, but Ajmal was no longer there. Getting down on his hands and knees, Raafe pushed aside grasses and felt the earth for signs. Nothing.

Returning to Naimah, Raafe brought her to his shoulder before deciding to hike the long way back to the makeshift hospital. He tried to keep his thoughts on helping the living and not on broken Tabani or missing Ajmal. Promising his cousins to come back, he tossed his coat over the lifeless Tabani.

*

Everywhere, the cries of the wounded and those who had lost someone dear rose up around Raafe and his unconscious cousin. What would he tell Naimah when she woke? How could he tell her that her son was missing and her sister gone?

Nurses and medics quickly moved from one patient to the next, trying to save as many lives as they possibly could. Raafe found the young medic Tariq, took him by the arm and pulled him toward the cot where he had laid his cousin. "Can you save her? Will she be all right?"

Tariq examined the gash in Naimah's head. She stirred for the first time and moaned. Both men stood back in surprise but smiled. "Yes," said Tariq, "but we don't have the medicines we need. Few supplies. You can see, however, she is breathing on her own. There are so many here who need more immediate attention."

"The baby, Ajmal was gone." Raafe hung his head and lowered his shoulders until he looked like an old man in the dim light.

"Don't give up hope," said Tariq. "He may yet be found. Make yourself useful and apply this dressing to her wound."

*

When she regained consciousness a day later, Naimah sat up, then stood too suddenly before nearly falling over. Raafe caught her. "Sit back down, please, cousin." He had slept only an hour during the long night.

"Ajmal? Where is my Ajmal?" Naimah's eyes were wide and her lips quivered slightly.

Raafe pulled her to him and held her while she sobbed. "Someone may yet find him," he said when she quieted.

"Then, his body has not been found?"

"No."

"We will find him," said Naimah suddenly standing straight and tall. Stopping her only for a moment, Raafe made her drink some water before they set out across the city and asked everyone about Ajmal.

No one could tell her anything about what happened except to say, "We are in a war. You are alive. You must go on." Strangers and distant relatives did not mean to be cruel, but prolonged wars have taken everything, leaving survivors without hope, even without compassion.

"You will bear other children," one old woman told her bitterly, having lost all her sons to wars.

Raafe knew, however, that his cousin could not forget her child. "We will keep looking," he said. "Someone is certain to have found him or seen something that can help us."

"We must search everywhere."

They returned to the temporary hospital to check amongst the wounded and dying.

Raafe and Naimah asked the doctors and nurses, looked at the children and babies who were injured until Naimah felt her eyes had been stung by wasps. Ajmal was not among them.

"How could they be so terrible?" Naimah asked no one in particular, but Raafe answered her.

"They know nothing now except fighting and killing." He was angry at his government, at the outside forces waging their proxy war in his land, at the groups resisting because that resistance only seemed to embolden other fighters. Raafe was angry with everyone at that moment except his injured cousin and his mother. If a soldier had walked through the door at that instant, Raafe thought he might kill the man, just out of pain and sorrow. He closed his eyes and breathed deeply. "No," he said out loud, reorienting himself. "I will not kill unless I have to do so," he reminded himself.

"What?" Naimah asked.

"Nothing. Nothing," he said.

"I want to go back to the road where you found me and Tabani."

"Naimah, I searched every inch of that road and the ground around it. Ajmal was not there. You must believe me."

With a ferocity he had seen only once before, Raafe knew it was useless to reason with his cousin. "All right. We'll look again."

*

Naimah led Raafe to the road where she and her sister were felled. Cousins searched the ground, carefully looking for signs that a baby had been there. They walked then crawled along, stood in the ditches at each side but could not find the child Ajmal, nor any indication of his presence.

"There is no body," said Raafe as he wiped the sweat from his forehead. "Perhaps someone found Ajmal and is taking care of him. If he was dead, there would be a body." Although Raafe was not sure if he believed what he said, he knew it was what his cousin needed to hear.

"There would be a body," she whispered to herself. She looked up at Raafe, pleadingly.

"Perhaps someone has taken him home and is being good to him. There are still good people among us."

His statement gave Naimah hope.

"If another woman found my baby," she said, her voice trailing off in that faith.

*

For days and weeks and months, Naimah continued her search, stopping other women and asking if they had saved a lost baby. She described Ajmal. "He has dark hair and long eyelashes, a pretty baby boy," she said. Then softly, "He looks like my father." Naimah realized how silly she sounded because most of these other women had never met nor seen her father who had been dead many years by that time. "He might be crying for me," she said at last. "Oh, and he has a tiny blue birthmark near his left eye." She chastised herself for not starting with this clue to finding her son. The other women gently patted Naimah on her back. They all knew loss with great familiarity.

Raafe finally had to leave his cousin in the company of other women to fight in the endless war himself. "They will not stop until every last one of us has been sacrificed," he said to his friend but not his mother, who would hold out hope for her son's return.

IV

Makram and Language Below Language

Life in the water was fine, but the tadpoles had all long ago hatched, and Ajmal's air and food bubble sometimes threatened to break. Ahura Mazda said to Ajmal, "You are getting too big for me to feed you this way. And I keep repeating my stories. We will have to find another caretaker for you soon, little one."

Now, it was most fortunate that Ahura Mazda knew other spirit creatures, and he beckoned Makram, a Wolf, with a loud CROOOAK. Makram had crossed over the border between countries, then moved into Perterra quite seamlessly a long time ago.

"How did you happen to arrive so quickly?" asked the frog as Makram gently pulled the baby from the water with his teeth and licked Ajmal's belly with his smooth, long tongue.

Ajmal giggled as the wolf tickled his wet skin. After snuggling next to the warm dry wolf, Ajmal immediately fell asleep.

"I saw you struggling from a mile away," said Makram. "Heard your complaints in your flattery of the boy. He's too big for you to care for now."

Sadly, yet with some degree of relief, Ahura Mazda had to admit the wolf was right. "Of course. Perhaps you can take over. He is a delightful human child but growing and eating more than I can provide. I would be most grateful if you would make this next stage of the expedition with him."

"What is my charge? How long? You knew, of course, that I had released another human back into mortal dimension not so very long ago. Why this child?"

"So many questions. Until he has outgrown your teachings and protection. This is one answer: this child—because he landed next to me. It is reason enough."

Makram coughed in the menacing way a wolf is apt to do. "Judging from the size of him, that will likely be a very long time."

"I would go further with him if I could, you understand."

"There are so many human children who need help and care, and yet, we have this one. If only men would take better care of their children."

"Stop complaining. He plopped in front of me. Dropped out of the sky and in the midst of my teachings to my young tadpoles. He who crossed over, you could say, he chose me rather than the other way around. But that is the way man's expanse bumps into ours sometimes, colliding with Perterra unexpectedly. I can't say I was pleased at first, but I have come to like this human. He smiles and burps almost as well as me."

At that moment, Ajmal released a loud burp, pleased with himself.

Makram pawed the dirt in front of him as the kicked his feet. "Look at him. He thinks he is still swimming. You have led him to believe he is a frog."

Frog and huge wolf laughed in the way that only creatures in Perterra are able, sounding relieved and pleased with one another and themselves. Finally, Ahura Mazda released a gas bubble as he was exiting. "Oh, and he stinks, too," said Makram.

Ahura Mazda gathered up the folds of his skin and said, "I must be going then if you have this under control."

"I will do my best, as you have done," said Makram. Ahura Mazda amused him, but the great wolf held the highest regard for the brilliant little frog.

"It is unlikely the human will remember me, but that is as it should be," said Ahura Mazda as he hopped away, disappearing into a shallow, green pool of water.

"Ajmal will remember you because I will tell this boy child how you cared for him," said Makram, more to himself than anyone because the baby had fallen back to sleep and the frog beyond hearing.

*

Within a short time, Makram had taught the little boy to eat mashed meat the wolf had first chewed thoroughly for him. In no time, the toddler grew strong and learned to ride on the wolf's back. It was easier on them both than being dragged in the mouth of the wolf. Ajmal held Makram's thick fur for balance and snuggled next to the wolf for warmth.

Makram remembered well man's violence and sometimes considered keeping Ajmal forever. The child slept in the deep blue-green woods, curled in the bristled fur of his protector, cooing softly.

Yet Ajmal dreamed and saw confusing images that slipped through his mind like running water. He recalled water, breathing water but confused his feelings of freedom with swimming and refused to share visions of that other land.

"You were dreaming," said Makram. "What was your dream?"

"I was running and chasing foolish rabbits," said Ajmal who had learned to speak and talk with Makram very early. The child lied, attempting to please his teacher and protector. Already, Ajmal discovered that lying could be a benefit to him.

"That was my dream, one I have told you. Why would you chase rabbits? You don't need to lie to me. You were flying in your dream."

"How did you know?"

"Your feet were not running, and your arms were spread wide, catching wind."

"You are right, but it was a sad dream."

"Not sad. Instructive and perhaps revealing something of your future."

"I will fly?" asked the excited boy.

"Dreams may reveal symbols or foreshadow what is to come. This dream of yours is a long way off, so we don't know yet."

As they approached a river, the child ran ahead and leaped into the water. After a minute, he emerged sputtering and coughing at the surface.

Makram shook his head. "You are not with the frog anymore. You must breath air, not water, remember."

"But I can swim." The child ducked his head again before rising, pushing himself along.

"Of course. Most men swim, too."

"Oh." Ajmal was hurt that he was not doing anything special, as Makram reminded him.

"Don't worry," said Makram. "You are still quite extraordinary. Otherwise Azura Mazda would not have spent so much of his time and energy keeping you alive."

"Azura Mazda?" Already, the little child had forgotten his frog protector, even his name.

"Oh, you have much to learn. Warm yourself in my fur and listen."

Ajmal ran to the wolf and threw his little arms around Makram's thick furry neck.

"Time for your studies." Makram taught Ajmal about Azura Mazda, about sacrifice and kindness, and then about languages and the language below language.

"How can I learn this other language?"

"You don't have to learn it. That language already exists inside; you have only to recognize it when you hear it again."

"Like what Ahura Mazda said to me when I was too young to talk?"

"Yes, and the language of your mother before you flew away."

V

Naimah Welcomed by Widows

"You are welcome to travel with us, to stay with us," Derifa said to Naimah as they rode in the wagon. After struggling to find an unthreatening place, Naimah was welcomed into a sisterhood of widows and orphan girls and women.

"Please, listen to us, Naimah." Several widows coaxed Naimah to leave with them. Encouraged after so much fear and terror, Naimah let her shoulders slump and leaned against the older woman in the back of a wagon as the group fled the fighting.

At first, she had resisted. "I can't leave. My baby may yet be alive."

"Then you will come back for him," Derifa said.

"If you stay here, you will be dead and no use to your son or anyone," another middle-aged woman said to her, leaning forward with her hands stretched toward Naimah. "If your baby is still alive, then someone is caring well for him."

"I will return for my son," she had said quietly, promising herself that she would never give up looking for her child. As the dusty road wore on, she began to think in terms of journeys, falling asleep and waking on the move.

At last they reached Jordan, and the group made their way to a Life Center where they were given food and medical attention. Two of the younger women were pregnant and worried for the babies they carried. Naimah helped the young women, offering part of her rations to them and giving up her blanket to cover them.

*

Sometime later, Felicidad entered the room and talked to the women about vocational classes. Few were interested in schooling, but the idea made Naimah curious. She moved to the front near Felicidad in the small, crowded apartment.

"You will be a good student," said Felicidad smiling at Naimah.

The words made Naimah feel a blessing for the first time in months. But there was a price to be paid for living in the shelter, and Naimah had much work to do.

In a short time, she found herself making soap to sell in exchange for food and shelter, the women banding together for protection and nourishment.

One of the women was very old and acted particularly kindly to Naimah. Kaheela told Naimah of her sorrows and listened as well as she spoke.

Kaheela, too, had lost her family, including her grown granddaughter.

"You will find your child someday, but you may not recognize him because he will be tall and strong, a man."

"You think I am not foolish then, believing he is still alive?" Naimah asked with some trepidation.

"You may be foolish, but it is a good kind," Kaheela said. "We all need such foolishness. I think you are right to believe your son is alive. Yes. I do. You told me they did not find his body, and who would not pick up a baby to help if she saw this babe alone near a road?"

"I'm sure they thought I was already dead if they could not wake me," Naimah said, feeling more hopeful than she had in many months. "I think you are right. Someone would have picked Ajmal up and loved him."

Other women joined them as they prepared the soap mixture. Naimah poured olive oil into liquid soap, then stirred. Intense fragrances rose up and made her eyes water. It was not an unpleasant smell at first but later began to nauseate her.

"You must stay strong and learn more, so you will be able to help your son once you find him," said Yara, adding water to the mixture and overhearing the conversation of Naimah and Kaheela.

"I will," said Naimah. "Your name, Yara, it means butterfly," she said, as Yara laughed lightly. "And Kaheela, your name means 'gift of God.'"

"Why do you know this?" asked Yara.

"I am always looking for meanings."

"My name should mean, suffered much and persisted," said Kaheela. She brought more oil to the women.

"You work so hard for all of us, and you have been through so much and have lived so long."

"Ah, yes, but Kaheela is a gift as you have said."

"I am not so well named," said Naimah, sprinkling in cinnamon and nigella seeds into the Nabulsi recipe. She did not mind long hours, but her feet ached after standing all day. "I will never be content and calm with my family lost or scattered. You said before that I might not recognize my son even if I find him. This is what makes me broken. What should I do?"

"Take your shattered heart and build. Build a tribute to your son. Perhaps he will then be able to find you some day."

"He will not know me either."

"It is in your nature to recognize one another. He will remember," Yara said, interjecting her ideas into the conversation between the other two.

Still disbelieving, Naimah said, "How can that be? He was separated from me before he could know me. He was too young to remember anything."

"Did he know you at his birth? Did he only quiet when you, over all others, held him?"

"Of course, he knew I was his mother."

"He knew before there is knowing. Your bond with your son is deeper than anything. Trust yourself and your love."

Naimah kept Yara's words in her heart and repeated them to herself at night.

*

After many months of making soap, Naimah began to take classes to educate herself. They were not university courses but simply schools for girls in which an instructor lectured to a roomful of young women and left books for them. She thought if she learned enough, she would be someday return to search for her son again.

Sharing her secrets with Kaheela, Naimah was concerned that her friend would be angry. "I am going to leave here soon," she said.

"You are either courageous or a fool, but if you must go, then go with my blessing," Kaheela answered.

"Perhaps I am a courageous fool."

"Go and find your place in the wide world. It is not here; it is not with us any longer."

"I will miss you. Once I was content to hold my husband with my right hand and my left hand over my belly where my son kicked inside me. All that comfort is gone."

"Where do you think you will go?"

"Perhaps to America."

"Why America? They are always hungry for battle, hold it in their bellies with want," Kaheela said with a quiver of accusation, her eyes darkening.

"No one can take away their desires for bloodlust, but I will show them one story of war."

"They will laugh at you. You are a poor Muslim woman who loves peace going to a Western country that produces conflict for profits," said Kaheela.

"It is likely they will never see me or notice what I write, but I must try."

"I don't understand. Travel to another city in our sphere. I will accompany you if you do not go far."

"But I must leave here in order to have a chance that they might listen. I will ask them to remember the interlude between fighting and smiles on the faces of their children. All people care about their children," said Naimah.

"I'm not so sure."

Both women looked up as birds gathered in a shifting mass, shapes charcoaled across the sky.

"They know something is about to happen," Kaheela said. "But not tonight. One last time, we will be together." The women hugged and fell asleep curled around one another.

Then came fire.

*

Losing her other family of women, Naimah nearly fell to the ground, unmoored, catching herself and passing through streets then cities as a perpetual foreigner, making no place a home. Her heart pounded in her throat, and she was afraid of everything for a time before she started writing in grief and anger. Gradually, anger gave way to detailed observation.

She had written about the women making soap and the men who harassed and frightened them. Her first story was about repetitive actions of making soap, soothing but not healing the harm done to each of the women who had fled wars and abuse. When she wrote this story, she reopened wounds with smoke and ash, concussive sounds emerging.

"Why write it if hurts you?" she could almost hear her dead sister Tabani asking.

"I do not want to forget. I will not forget you."

Naimah's words caught the attention of an editor who accepted the story for publication. Cities followed cities in orange, bright reds at night, a faint odor of burning in the air, Naimah's eyes watering at the rising sun and lengthening distance of memories.

VI

Baltasar and Ajmal Roam Perterra

As Ajmal grew tall, Makram, his wolf protector, turned to him and said, "It is time for you to learn from someone stronger than me, come."

"Who could be stronger than you?" asked Ajmal, incredulous.

"There is one stronger than me, and one stronger than him. Understand your gifts but remain humble."

"Will humility make me strong?"

"There are many kinds of strengths and having humility is one," Makram said. Before they went further, Makram nuzzled the lad in a rare display of both affection and regret. It would not be easy for the huge wolf to leave this particular human child.

*

Traveling deep into a dense, Perterra forest together, Ajmal was introduced to a great brown bear, Baltasar. "This fat old oaf will give you what you need to continue your journey and help you see and understand things I cannot. I must go now," Makram said.

"Take care with your compliments, wolf," growled Baltasar. Makram laughed in the way wolves do, the smile cutting across his muzzle.

Ajmal was still a boy, so he started to cry at the thought of losing his greatest companion and protector. "No tears," said Makram. "Life is ever-changing. Accept Baltasar's offering with gratitude and be ready for your next adventure. But you will not be forgotten, gentle boy." The great wolf turned again to Ajmal. "Keep reading. Never stop learning."

Ajmal buried his face in Makram's thick, warm fur. "I don't want you to leave," said the boy, sniffing back tears. "I will miss you too much."

"That is good. Remember what others have done for you, but do not be sad. Now, you begin your training with the great brown bear. Baltasar is my friend. He will become your friend, as well." With those words, Makram leaped into tall grasses, only once more looking back at the boy who had filled his life for those wondrous years. Makram, too, felt sorrow, but he could not let the boy know.

Ajmal stood looking into waving oceans of grass where Makram had disappeared. "Every time he leaves, I get a little choked up," said Baltasar. Ajmal studied the big bear for a moment.

"He told me about you, about how amazing you are and how you are searching to return to your original home. I can't imagine. It must be hard.

Unlike Makram and Azura Mazda, I have only known Perterra and wouldn't want to leave."

Ajmal said nothing in response, feeling as if he would burst into tears.

"Don't feel like you have to make conversation with me. I always talk a lot when I get nervous, and I get nervous when someone is depending upon me to know just what to do."

"You don't know what to do?" Ajmal was genuinely surprised at Baltasar's confession.

"Well, yes and no. I understand that I am to help you in your studies, but I don't really know how to get you back to the realm of men. I probably shouldn't have said that, but I get ridiculously honest when I'm uncertain."

"Makram always told me that honesty was a good quality."

"Oh, I'd never argue with Makram, and he's right, of course. But sometimes, a little less blinding truth is rather nice." Baltasar suddenly laughed, shaking everything around him, his brown fur suddenly thicker.

Ajmal smiled, thinking of times he would have liked to have stretched the truth, particularly when Makram asked if he had read every chapter in his book.

"I'm very large and loud, so I'll try my best to listen carefully when you speak. I'm working at hearing you right now."

"But I wasn't saying anything," said Ajmal.

"You weren't? Maybe I mistook that bird for your voice."

"A bird?" Ajmal looked around and saw several flying very high over them. "How could you have heard them?"

"I concentrate and quiet my busy mouth for a moment. They are all telling us something important."

Sounds of birds and flying insects producing a whir of urgency Ajmal knew was meant for him. But he was afraid if he heard everything, he would hear nothing. He decided to open his tender heart and told this fear to Baltasar.

"It is good you are able to hear the smallest sounds in life, but sometimes, you must focus only on what you need to hear, just one note. What important notes do you remember?" asked Baltasar.

Without realizing it and without understanding, Ajmal had already practiced listening only to Makram and pulses of life. He suddenly remembered a sound from before, an electric current that passed through him when he was too young to associate one thing with another. At that moment, he began to draw a picture of a world.

"There was another heart—like mine but not mine," he told Baltasar, confused about the impulse and what he was suggesting.

"Yes. Your protector Makram."

"No, this was not Makram whom I know as well as but distinctly from myself."

"Then our journey will be your preparation to understand that other heart—your own as well as one you do not yet recognize."

*

Baltasar lifted Ajmal with one paw, boy riding on the wide shoulders of that brown bear. As they tore through brush and past trees, over rocks and creeks, Ajmal let out a whoop of joy. Never had he covered so much ground so quickly and effortlessly. This bear was, indeed, stronger than Makram. Still, Ajmal missed his long-time wolf companion. He told all this to Baltasar.

"It is good—your whoop," said Baltasar. "You must find happiness even in sorrows." The great bear stopped for a moment to drink from a blue-green river. Ajmal followed him and bent down to lap cool water.

"You drink like a bear," laughed Baltasar.

"How should I drink then?"

"Scoop the water with your hands."

Ajmal clumsily tried but allowed all the water to escape through his fingers before getting any.

"It's too hard," he said, putting his face back in the water.

"Try again. Remember, your hands are a great advantage once you have mastered their use." Ajmal made several more attempts before he was successful.

"I did it," he yelled, then changed the topic, thinking about his differences from his animal guides. "Will men ever find peace in their world?"

"That remains to be seen, Ajmal. It is in the hands of men, in your hands, too, and your mother's."

"My mother's? Who is she?"

"I think it is time for you to know some of her story, but you must be hungry. So, first, we will get back quickly and put something in your belly. Hang on." Baltasar scooped up Ajmal and bolted off with him once again. As he bounded, Baltasar told the story of a woman who was looking for her son for many years. This woman searched in sorrow but never without hope. "After picking herself up, she began her long trek on a road toward awakening men to the need for peace. Your mother, you see, never gave up hope of finding you."

VII

Another Dangerous Man

If Abhimanya had not tried to kill her by setting fire to their house, Naimah might have stayed with her many adopted sisters longer. Only later could she recall that terrible night of the fire.

Naimah was aware of this sullen man following her but did not think he posed a real danger at first. After making and selling soap all day, Naimah noticed the heavy-set, brooding man coming too close. Each day, he would be waiting, and she had to hurry to avoid his contact. Twice, he had reached out and nearly touched her as she moved quickly to rejoin her sisters.

One morning, he walked up behind her and shouted his name. "Abhimanya. What is yours? I will buy whatever you want. Come with me."

Naimah shook her head. "I am not looking for a husband," she said, moving away quickly and adroitly.

With his thick brows tightly knit, he scolded, "I want you. Let me take you or no man will. It is your choice."

"Then it will be no man," she answered too bravely. Just then, several of her friends came out to greet her, and Abhimanya hesitated before backing up angrily, cursing, his hands moving involuntarily into fists.

Naimah turned once to see him look at her with such hatred it startled her again. When she thought about the man who followed her, she remembered his name Abhimanya means "short-tempered" and decided it would be best to avoid him by taking alternate routes to the shop.

*

When he thought Naimah was in her bed sleeping with the other women, Abhimanya set fire to the house where they lived together. Naimah and many of her sisters had worked later than usual that night and were not yet home when Abhimanya lit papers and kindling in an alley next to their building. He felt justified in his revenge, watching flames grow and leap about, catching new life with each ember. He lurked nearby while firemen came, and a few old women ran out crying and screaming. Only one woman, who had been sick for weeks, never woke before the smoke from the fire choked her.

Nowhere did Abhimanya see Naimah in that small group of frightened women huddling together outside waiting for the fire to be extinguished. He lurked about, sneaking behind one building then another to look for her. He both hoped she was dead and that she would come screaming out of the fires toward him. Too many people crowded around, and Abhimanya had to leave the area before seeing Naimah. He would return in the morning, he told himself.

Police began investigating the death of the woman who did not make it out during the fire. They were asking questions and taking descriptions, and Abhimanya had to flee that part of the city. He was a bully and a murderer, as Naimah knew, but Abhimanya was also a great coward as bullies often are.

*

Comforting her sisters with whom she had made soap and grown to love, Naimah said, "I do not know what I will find, but I must continue on my journey." For a long time, Naimah had been wondering if she and her sister Tabani should have stayed in the bombed out building instead of fleeing along the road on that fateful night. Would Ajmal be with her still? Would Tabani be alive? Regret flooded her thoughts at night until sleeping became impossible. At last, she decided that leaving was the only way she could keep from going mad.

After tears and hugging, women offered her what little they had in coins, kissed her cheeks, and watched her until she disappeared.

*

Arriving in an airport, Naimah stood looking out a window, watching planes land and take off, her eyes moving between outside and inner landscapes, following first the flight of small birds darting in and out of steel rafters above her head. A child wandered away from his parents, and Naimah went over to direct him back to his mother.

"Where did you go?" a mother asked, embarrassed. "He's always wandering off like that."

"Don't leave your mother's side," said Naimah scolding the boy, before walking down a long hallway that led to gates of planes arriving and leaving. There would always be lost children, but she could not stand by and do nothing. Feeling in her pocket, she was relieved to touch her ticket purchased by owners of the apartment building that burned. They were cited for many violations and settled with small sums to pay off the women who survived. Naimah discovered their generosity was not really generous. Although arson was the culprit, the fire would not have been so effective if the landlord had kept up with repairs and removed rubbish in an alley and near the entrance and exit as so often promised.

Naimah's plane ticket was to another city by the sea where a hotel had inquired about hiring women to clean and serve. She worked as a maid and housekeeper when she arrived. Even during all her time making soap and then cleaning hotel rooms, she always told stories to herself, tales of people she had known, and how her world could be rather than what it was.

*

A blond woman with gold earrings and bracelets, summoned Naimah to poolside to fetch her a drink. It was not Naimah's job, but she brought the woman her cocktail. "You poor thing," said this wealthy woman. "You look uncomfortably hot. You must wish you could dive in and take off that nasty headscarf. Does the help ever have an opportunity to find a place to swim? Do you get a chance even to bathe?" Such questions seemed to be the same for so many of the rich, thinking their privilege was deserved and not a trick of fate.

"We do," said Naimah.

The wealthy woman lost interest in Naimah temporarily, waving to another rich woman who would join her in gossiping about their wealthy husbands and occasional lovers. But the rich woman did not entirely forget about Naimah and asked her what she wished for in return for the little extravagances she had brought.

"I would like to leave this country."

"You need a Visa? I happen to know someone in the foreign office," the rich woman said, smiling. She loved doing little favors for her help. It made her feel even more superior.

*

Folding washed linens, Naimah then began to prepare her strong coffee. Sitting down and inhaling fragrances of the same coffee the wealthy drank, she noticed a lizard scaling a nearby wall. Creature stopped as if to tell her something then scurried off, its hesitate movements reminding her of something distant, something never fully realized on a night she ran from war with her son. When Naimah finished her coffee, she returned to her work until dark, all the while filling her head with her compositions. Words flowed around her and pulled back waves in a cooling sea.

*

The first time she went down to the water, waves mesmerized her, thundering in, rumbling, crashing, rolling back, water renewing like hope. Naimah saw a black, humped shape off shore, a fin disappearing before animal registered as dolphin. Dolphins rose again, further out, before descending to unseen depths she could not imagine.

"Is my son with you, dolphin?" she asked in a whispered prayer before venturing closer, allowing her feet to touch water. This prayer was offered before she had left her faith drowning in waters of sorrow. In its place, doubt and courage entered and settled into her nature. She imagined more stories and how she would write them all down.

Walking along shoreline, Naimah saw a line of gulls punctuating lines in the sea like periods in a sentence. White gulls were sentries who had forgotten vigilance and become fascinated with their own writings in the sky.

Near a pier, a boy fished off a rock outcropping. As she approached, Naimah imagined he was about 10 years, the same age as her son would be if he had not been lost to her. Twenty-feet away, she stopped again and watched the boy cast his line into surf, again and again. His stroke was easy and natural as if he had been a fisherman before birth, and she knew then this child could not be her son.

VIII

Ajmal Discovers Man's Violence

"There are too many wars, Baltasar," said Ajmal suddenly, putting down his history text. "Why must human beings be so violent and unrelentingly cruel?"

"Not all men or women are violent and cruel," responded the bear as he scratched behind his ears. "Yet, war does seem inevitable for them unless something changes."

"Why? Couldn't they make another choice? Those who are not violent should persuade violent ones, shouldn't they? It is not logical to go on killing endlessly."

Baltasar laughed with his fur rippling. "For you, there is always an answer. I like that about you, boy."

"Shouldn't there be an answer to everything?"

Baltasar pondered then said, "Yes, but there are often too many answers that conflict with one another."

"Why can't the world of men be clearer like it is here in Perterra?"

"Ah, we are not so many here. I'm happy just to run into another soul after many days away. Maybe if we were all on top of one another, like they are in the world you came from, we would fight and argue here, too."

"If violence is an inevitability with contact, why should I read and study? What is the point of trying to learn?" Ajmal threw a stone into the air and watched as it disappeared. "What happened to that stone?"

Baltasar looked up and shrugged. "You and your questions? You make my head ache," said Baltasar, putting an enormous paw to his head. "Always there is a book in your hands and a question on your mind."

"But it was you and my other mentor—"

"Mentors. Don't forget Ahura Mazda."

"I was a baby then. I'm afraid I have forgotten—"

"You should still remember him even if we must paint the pictures for you."

"It was my mentors who gave books to me."

"Of course, you should read and learn. I'm not saying there are not answers, but there are many complications. Yes, you should question. I'm afraid I'm not as smart as Ahura Mazda or Makram," said the great brown bear, looking a bit forlorn. Then an idea occurred to him: "Sometimes there is no one answer, just different possibilities and alternate ways of framing."

"Like which author is best?" Ajmal jumped up on a rock and spread his arms out wide.

"Exactly. Don't fall off."

"I won't." Ajmal pretended to trip and caught himself, laughing.

"Ah, what will I do with you? Each group will argue over their own bests without even considering greats from other lands. Territorial."

"This is frustrating," said the boy, climbing down. "The more I read, the more ignorant I feel I have become. How will I ever be able to help others when I will never know enough?"

"You are truly acquiring wisdom. Just knowing that you don't know everything already makes you smarter than many of the men you will one day meet. Only wise men understand that there is so much beyond any one man's reach." As Baltasar spoke, he dipped a paw into a stream and effortlessly caught a fat, silver fish.

"I wish I could catch them as easily as you."

"I am the better fisherman for now, but you may learn how to create implements that will allow you to catch far bigger fish someday."

"How big?"

"Bigger than you. Bigger even than me."

"Such fish really exist in their dominion?"

"In oceans on Earth, there are fish as long as that tree." Both stopped to consider the size of such gargantuan imagined fish.

"Will you think me a coward if I say that frightens me?"

Baltasar rose to his full height which sometimes still surprised Ajmal. "Do not fear those who are larger than you," said Baltasar. "They may fall more easily." With that, Baltasar dropped down again and comforted the 13-year old. "We have a fish to eat to make us stronger."

"I want you to live forever," Ajmal said worried for his companion.

"Everything leaves at some point. It is natural even in Perterra."

"How will I ever find my way once you are gone?"

"It is not you who are lost but your sphere that has lost you. Remember what you have learned and be only as brave as you have already been." Baltasar bit off the head of the fish and swallowed. Then he extended his paw holding a clean slice of the fish. Ajmal took it and bit off a chunk, chewing hard.

"How will I know when to cross? Where I will come out?"

"We wait until a thinning, and someone or something will pull you back into that other terrene you will soon want."

"How do you know I will ever want that other place? I don't. I am quite happy here." Ajmal looked around him at swirling blues and deep green mists, colors overlapping and swallowing one another as in an abstract painting. "Why would I leave my friends to go to a warring dimension?"

"Because you are needed there."

"You don't need me here?"

Baltasar puzzled over the boy's question. "I don't know about all of Perterra, but I think I might need you now."

Ajmal ran at the great bear and buried himself in his fur. "I am only an insignificant boy. How can I change anything?"

Baltasar hesitated. "You are only one, but you have changed me."

"I am too small," said Ajmal, uncertain.

"Ah, by now, you must know size is a relative quality. You are more than large enough to make a difference. Sometimes a small shift will alter the course of an entire planet. And it is nearing your time. I must introduce you to your next teacher, Shadi." Quite suddenly, it seemed, a wild goat appeared and leaped down from a nearby rock above them.

"Where did you come from?" Ajmal asked, innocently and surprised because he thought he was keenly observant.

"I have always been here. On that rock there. It is you who finally decided to look up and notice me."

"You think I should want to find my way back?" Ajmal asked, turning to Baltasar, who was turning away, leaving him in the care of the goat.

"Baltasar? Baltasar?" asked Ajmal, a quiver in his voice.

"Do not be sad, and do not break my very large heart," said Baltasar, bounding back to embrace the child. "This little goat will be a fine teacher, likely a better teacher even than me."

"Of course. I am to be your mentor and friend. Look forward and come along. We have much to learn," said Shadi, impatient to get started on their journey.

Baltasar reluctantly let the boy go and bounded off into the wood, knocking down the grasses and brush in his path.

"No!" yelled Ajmal forlornly, looking after the disappearing brown bear.

"Oh, dear, oh, dear," said Shadi. "I'm not fully prepared for your sadness and protests. I promise to be a good guide and instructor."

"But I have learned so much already. What more would you have me do?" Ajmal turned again to look for Baltasar. "Will he come back?"

"I don't know. He's not there now. Don't despair. I would have you know all things that men do not understand. Literature and history, philosophy, and science are a beginning, but you must dig deeper. And I will guide you."

"How will you help? You are not as wise as Makram or as strong as Baltasar."

"I, my dear boy, am a balladeer. Shadi at your service. It is my pleasure to sing histories, stories, poems, and the tales of humans and beasts that touch your soul. Music and art will change you and others. Let me warm up my vocal cords for a moment. Lalala la."

Dismissing the singing goat, Ajmal said, "I'm not sure I want to return to that earthly setting, as Baltasar said I would. Maybe I won't go. Maybe I will go off and find Baltasar."

"It is natural that you would rebel, too. You have learned enough by now to know men can be a plague," said Shadi. "Yet, something stronger than any of us will draw you back. You are, after all, a man."

"I am a man?"

"Not quite yet. I meant you belong in the realm of men."

Ajmal frowned at Shadi's correction. "Am I not a plague then, as well?"

"While you are not yet a man, you are certainly no plague. Just remember those sad eyes of Baltasar as he left. You apparently have considerable charm and value."

"I am close to being a man. I don't want to be part of their plague."

"Then you will not be. Every man has a choice. Not all men are awful. There are millions of good ones. Maybe more. Mathematics—not my strong point."

"Men are destructive. Why didn't Baltasar attack me while it was easy for him? Get rid of this plague. I would not even fight him. Why would he want to help a man return to other violent men? Why are you willing to help me?"

"Baltasar did not fight you because there was no need. He could easily have defeated you, but then what? Men do not yet understand that the stronger beast does not need to fight to prove anything. There is another reason, too."

"Tell me," demanded Ajmal.

"You are a chosen child. One we are to educate and assist, so that some possibility of peace still may exist for man. But, at any rate, it is too late to talk about Baltasar. I'm tasked with your education, and you still have much to learn. I am a singer by nature, as I mentioned."

"Songs? How can singing help me or anyone?"

"Histories and poetry of man are written in song. If given a choice between fighting and singing, always choose singing. But you have time to figure this out."

"I already know about the ways of men. I have read and studied their history and wars, their many religions and anger, their irrational fears and violence. I know them too well through all I have read."

"What do you know? Whose history? Victors or the defeated? From what perspective were your texts written? Even if you have some rudimentary grasp of human past as recorded by certain groups, you do not know their future or even a true representation of their past."

"No one can know the future."

"Don't be too sure."

"I already know more than enough."

"Be careful. Hubris and too much certainty often play a role in man's downfall."

"Why must I consider what has not yet happened?"

"Because you have a free will to act. You may act to help others or only yourself. You may prevent tragedies or contribute to them. Without forethought and divergent thinking, men's cities will crumble and flood or burn. All will be water or ash. All lost in water just as man was born out of water. All lost in flames from which the phoenix is born." Shadi leaped up a pile of rocks, and Ajmal struggled to climb behind him. "Come, come. You are a slowpoke. I saw you leaping earlier. I know you can do better."

"I'm not as nimble as a goat, but I have resolve and courage. What was that about Earth flooding or burning? Perterra, too?"

"Men do not listen to scientists who tell them about their awful contributions to altering terrain. Their ignorance and greed will be the death of them and many more innocents when rains and floods arrive. They burn their own cities in warring."

Ajmal suddenly stopped, remembering tales Makram had told him about Azura Mazda and his infancy. "Well, if I must return to a fire or flood, it is good I already know how to swim."

"Hah. You know how to make me laugh. That is a start."

"Why would cities burn if floods are coming? Won't rains put out fires?"

"When there is not enough land for men to retreat, wars over land not covered by water will destroy both our realms."

Looking very serious then, Ajmal asked, "Why here, too? You have nothing to do with them."

"We have everything to do with mankind, unfortunately or fortunately, depending upon your perspective."

"If we are connected, why can't I just walk back onto their land?"

"You are not ready yet, and you have not noticed the path or you would not need me at all." Ajmal leaned his head out, looking right and left for a hidden path, seeing nothing. "Not yet," said Shadi. "Soon enough, that is exactly what you will do."

"There is no map to follow. How will I know when I have arrived?"

"Trust yourself, and trust me and Baltasar and Makram," said Shadi. "We didn't take you all this way for nothing." A rock wall rose up before them, and blue-gray mists lifted boy and goat to the top without any further effort on their part.

"We are on top of a mountain."

"That we are. Lalala."

"I would rather trust myself or Baltasar. I can barely hear you when you're not singing."

"You must listen for sounds below your loud human voice." Just then, they both looked up at a flock of birds moving above them.

"I envy migrating birds and beasts," Ajmal said. "Their instincts tell them where to go, and when they must return. I have no such gifts."

"Envy no creature. Respect them all. You have gifts yet to be discovered. If they were near enough to visit with you, it is likely the birds would tell you how fortunate you are."

"How should I act when I come across other men?"

"As yourself. Remember, it is your world, too. At first, their horns, explosions, their awful clang and clatter of human activity, even outside of war, will be nearly deafening, but you will adjust. Don't panic. Remind yourself, what you know, and who you are." Perterra's blue-gray winds swirled around them, bringing them gently to the base of the mountain on the other side.

"I would rather stay here than return, as you and Baltasar say I must."

"That can never be. Whether we wish it or not, your destiny lies as a mortal man. In time, you will be ready. Now for your lessons. I will begin singing in Spanish then move into French, finishing with flourish, as I always do, in unrhythmic English."

"Why English?"

"I'm told you will arrive in America, New York, specifically. I've never been there, but we can study together. They mostly speak English there, but your Spanish will help you, too."

"How do you know these things?"

Instead of answering, Shadi began singing as he leaped from rock to rock.

*

IX

Naimah Writes

Naimah read and studied, surprised to discover there was so much to know in the universe. With each new concept she read about, she felt the sting of her ignorance and determined to take away that pain with new knowledge. At first, information came from old books, those cast off by others and free for her to take and study. Later, when pages were torn and injured from use, she began to write her own ideas and thoughts in margins. When there was not enough room, she wrote over existing words, her own supplanting those of another. Yet, she thought of the process as adding to the whole.

Every line she created carried weight of memory, of her son, her sister and husband. Naimah knew now that she had once lived simply and had only a desire to take care of her child Ajmal, her sister Tabani, and her husband Nabil.

"You do not need to listen to our words, our politics," Nabil had told her when she stood in the doorway, hesitating to come into the presence of the men arguing. "This is nothing that concerns you," he stood up and told her, turning her away after she served them strong coffee. "These are long and deep hatreds." He shook his head then suddenly smiled weakly. "No harm will ever come to you," he said with conviction, gently touching the top of her hijab and kissing her forehead. It was an act of love she now recognized but also a dismissive one.

Within a month, Nabil and her father Saad were gone forever. In looking back, Naimah tried to imagine where they were, what had happened in those final moments of their shortened lives.

*

The long line on the page was her son's time in her womb when she spoke to him before anyone in their house was awake, his foot jutting out, pushing against her skin, thin membrane separating while also connecting them.

"You're as big as a house," Tabani had once told her, laughing. "Don't eat so much."

"I want my son to grow strong and healthy."

"At this rate, your son will emerge too big even for his father to handle." They both smiled, thinking of the boy who would enrich their lives.

Those were her good days, Naimah thought, and they were so few she could still count them on her fingers.

*

    She read English and American authors, as well as Middle Eastern ones, coming across Ta-Nehisi Coates as if he was an old friend in, *We Were Eight Years in Power*. When he wrote, "The warlords of history are still kicking our heads in, and no one, not our fathers, nor our Gods, is coming to save us," she felt the barb as if it was still hooked into her skin. What does it say of us, of our religions, that we can outgrow all of them? If nothing is coming to save us, then we must save ourselves, Naimah thought. Yet, she secretly hoped someone was looking out for her lost son.

    She had never been in a position of power. Her range of vision opened and reopened again, each time exploding all her misconceptions and formerly held beliefs. "Knowledge is like an exploding star," she wrote to her old friend Kaheela, "a brilliant light is produced but at the expense of all that came before, destroying orbs of thought as new ones are created." Naimah wondered if Kaheela would be frightened by her words.

    Kaheela never answered her letters, but Naimah knew Kaheela would not have paper and pen, would be unsure of her command of language to write a letter. Still, Kaheela would welcome letters because she would then know that Naimah had not forgotten her.

*

    After many years, Naimah had made her way across the Atlantic to America. She had been fortunate to work for a woman who was generous, giving her raises and paying her well. Not every employer was good to her, but Naimah never forgot those acts of generosity ladled out with the occasional cruelty. She hoped to someday repay that woman in a small way. At last, Naimah had enough saved for a passage to America. She had begun to dream of a better life and was coaxed by the descriptions of this land of people mixing from all over the world. Her dream of America had yet to meet the reality of the people in this country across a deep ocean.

    When she landed, she sought out others who would know her language, so she could relax just a little when she spoke. But, always, she continued to challenge herself and write in English to reach that larger audience of what had been the most powerful nation. Curled in her dormitory bed in an apartment with many other immigrant women, Naimah felt little comfort in their presence. They, too, were frightened and often silent.

    One night, Naimah heard a soft sobbing coming from a bunk near hers. She crawled out of bed and knelt by the bed of the other woman.

"Why are you crying?"

"I've made a terrible mistake coming here. I know no one, and everyone looks at me like I'm a monster. I'm a fool. I will die alone."

Naimah lay on the bed with the young woman and held her, stroked her dark hair, and whispered to her. "You will see; it will turn out fine for you. Don't fear. Leave that behind." At last the young woman stopped shuddering and slept, but Naimah kept her wide-open eyes fixed on a spot on the ceiling where the pipes crossed over one another, water occasionally dripping on the beds.

In the morning, Naimah determined to improve her education and took the young woman with her. Together they enrolled in a city college course.

"How will I ever pay for this?" asked the woman. Naimah took her to the financial aid office, and they sat down to create a plan. Within a few days, however, the other woman had decided not to go back or pay for her course. She found work in a kitchen.

Feeling unseen and unheard in such a great and busy city, Naimah continued her writings and took another college course.

"Will you study astronomy then?" asked a fellow student and Syrian immigrant after their class.

"No, I only wish to know the stars, so I better understand our limitations."

"What is this you are working on, then? This idea called 'Newton's Mountain?' I saw your notes."

"Ah, I'm no expert, only a child touching her toes in milky waters of our universe, but I think that Newton was describing how fast an object must move in order not to be pulled to earth by gravity."

"I'm not sure I understand," said Rima.

"Newton theorized that if you could shoot an object from a cannon setting atop the highest mountain, the object would fall more gradually, depending upon the speed with which it was shot out into the atmosphere." Naimah expressed this concept visually, as well, using her hands and arms as object and mountain. "If an object was moving fast enough from high enough, then that object might never touch ground because earth is curving away at the same rate the object is falling, due to gravitational pull. This object, then, would continue to orbit, much like our moon. All of this was termed a thought experiment."

"You know so much, Naimah. I cannot keep up with you."

"I know less than when I began my studies." The friends were silent for several moments as they walked.

Then, sensing the sadness behind her friend's eyes, Rima asked, "Do you still hope to find your son?"

"Walking down a street, I sometimes think I see him coming toward me. The young man approaches, but then passes me. I realize this Middle Eastern man who started then stared at me with hostile eyes is only a stranger. Averting my gaze, I look down, not in shame or deference, but so he will not see my sorrow. But I will keep looking even though my odds of ever finding him are too terrible to consider."

"I'm sorry you cannot find your son. How is it that you still have hope?"

"When it rains here, the scene can seem suddenly familiar, before foreignness is distinct again. I take comfort in small things."

"That does not answer my question. Do you still hope? Is finding your son your own Newton's Mountain, thought experiment?"

"Perhaps. I only know that I must keep open the possibility, just as I try to imagine an environment in which peace one day may be achieved."

"Peace on this planet? Now, I know you are a little crazy." Rima laughed. "But I'm glad I know you."

"It is the only answer I have for you or myself."

*

Naimah was clear-eyed when she told the stories of the women she had known. They were simple tales, but a New York magazine editor liked them and published one of the tales, and then a second one was published in an online magazine. One thing followed another in fortunate drops of good luck.

A grant, a happenstance, and a woman who bestowed gifts from her post, lifted Naimah from serving in the cleaning industry and allowed her more time to think and write, to read, speculate, imagine, and to continue to hope.

X

Viper Faraj Instructs

"See how easily you have mastered Arabic," said Shadi to Ajmal.

"It seems to come naturally," said Ajmal, shrugging his narrow shoulders. He mastered Arabic and suspected the language was in his blood even before Shadi told him he had been born to an Arab woman.

"Tell me more about her." Ajmal stopped and called ahead to Shadi. "Come back. Wait. Tell me."

"Stop demanding and listen," said Shadi although he did return to the tall boy becoming man. "When the time is right, you will know."

"I will? What will I know? That I have returned to their world? That I have found my mother? Is this possible?"

"Anything and everything are possible but not likely."

"Then why prepare me for something so unlikely? I know so little about her. Even if I returned to man's environs, how would I discern in which direction to turn? Surely, my mother has not stayed in one place so long. You said I will land near her, but suppose my mother is in Syria or Lebanon or some other country where I do not know how to reach her? There are too many people on Earth to find her. Can you at least give me her name?"

"You know much more than you realize, but to discover her, you must quiet yourself and your fears. Be observant. Read signs. Remember, she is looking for you, as well."

Ajmal subconsciously touched the blue birthmark near his eye. "Not an answer but a riddle. I ask you only for her name."

"Her name is Naimah."

"Naimah? And?"

"So, now you are finally quiet. No more questions?"

"No. Suppose I land in front of my mother by some strange coincidence that you have arranged, but she does not recognize me? I am grown."

"She will know you. And if you were to land near her, it would be part of a grand design of which I have a part so small as to be insignificant."

"You are definitely not insignificant but very quick. Could you slow down with your leaping? Remember, I am not a mountain goat."

"How could I forget?"

"Even if my mother is somehow still alive, if men are so terrible, why should I return?"

"Your world is not terrible, just in need of many adjustments. If, and I must add this qualifier, if you were to somehow find your way back to the realm of your birth, you will find much to love, as well."

"It is not my world. I belong here."

"Only for a time."

"What should I listen for? Something or someone not present? It all seems impossible," said Ajmal impatiently even as he suspected he had heard this story before.

"By now you should be comfortable with impossibility—like possibilities are states of mind." Shadi began singing in French. "What did you think of my poem?"

Because he was uncomfortable and felt foolish as well as impatient, Ajmal wanted to change subjects. "Why should I know so many languages? French? This is all too difficult. My mind is already full. Of what use is all of this?"

"Your mind will never be full. The nature of man is hard but nearly limitless. You must be prepared. You never know exactly where your quest will lead you. Besides, French is beautiful. Just listen."

*

"It is time for your new mentor, my young friend," said Shadi to Ajmal as they caught their breaths at the bottom of a rock ledge.

"What? So soon? Maybe I'm not ready yet. I was finally getting used to you." Ajmal scratched his chin in nervous anticipation. He felt a prickling sensation as the first hairs appeared on his chin.

"And I was getting used to your endless questions, but these are not matters I can change."

"Why not? Let's just say we prefer to stay together for a while longer."

Shadi leaped up on the ledge. Ajmal quickly scrambled up after him. "You're more agile than you used to be," Shadi said with obvious pride. "Someone has taught you well."

"And you're no humbler than me."

Shadi brayed with laughter.

"I can stay up with you, and I promise not to hold you back ever again."

"Oh, Ajmal, my dear boy, don't misunderstand. I don't want to leave you. This change is for your own good, and I suspect for your mother, too."

"My mother again? I don't even know her. Why speak of her?"

"You didn't know me a year ago, and look how we've gotten along. You have to trust me on this. Now look down behind that clump of grass between those two rocks. You will find your next travel companion."

Lifting his mottled, pale gray and pink, triangular shaped head from the desert floor, the Levantine, blunt-nosed viper Faraj studied the tall youth in front of him.

"Oh," said Ajmal, surprised. "This snake is to be my mentor?"

Faraj did not speak but studied the youth by raising his head and body higher.

"Never discount potential contributions of others," said Shadi, growing sad and no longer trying to hide it.

Ajmal turned to Shadi again. "Couldn't you both be my guides? Why do you have to leave? I'm not sure a snake can—"

"That is the way in Perterra, and why our friendships are so deep. We understand well their impermanence." Shadi rubbed his forehead against Ajmal's hip. "Now watch your step and listen to Faraj. He is wiser than he looks." With that, Shadi leaped two rocks at a time and was nearly out of sight. Ajmal followed him with his eyes to the top of the mountain.

After moments of sorrow, Ajmal turned to examine the snake again. "I won't step on you, don't worry."

"Perhaps it is you who should be worried," replied Faraj. "My bite is laced with poison. But, let us leave off boastful and unnecessary threats. We know that neither of us will hurt the other. It is nearing the time for your rebirth into the physical, man-dominated sphere."

"Your name? It means 'truth?' Is that why you are so blunt?"

"I prefer the term honest. I will tell you my assessment of any situation as best and as fully as I am able."

"I am ready for the changes ahead." Ajmal couldn't help turning to glance over his shoulder to see if he could catch one more glimpse of Shadi, but the wise old goat was gone.

"I expect you are, seeing that you have nearly grown to my length and know that other environment well, if only from books. I also see you are brave and curious, even if a bit foolish. You will need every ounce of that bravery in this new realm you seek."

"I'm not so sure I am seeking man's world. This is my mentors' idea, and while we're discussing my better qualities, I am unlikely ever to lose them since they were given to man as a curse, not a gift. What would you have me learn now? I can't help feeling I already know it all."

"You know it all? A little more humility wouldn't hurt."

"Ah, all of my companions have suggested that I tamp down my pride in my knowledge. But I have worked so hard for it. Yet, I must assume you are right." For the first time, Ajmal felt rebellious and ready to strike out on his own. He was beginning to grow weary of the new mentors turning up.

"It's a start. Never underestimate others, but you also don't have to assume they are correct in whatever they are telling you. Sadly, you will need to learn suspicion. And I, apparently, am the best mentor to teach you skepticism."

"A skill I will also need among men?"

"Most definitely. And, by the way, your curiosity is not a curse, as you say, but means of discovery. Now, let's discuss philosophy. What do you know about mankind's search for answers?"

"Philosophy or religion. I know a lot! No, wait. Let me try again. I know a little but, perhaps, enough to discuss the subjects with you, at least adequately, if not well."

"Much better, Ajmal. Humility first. You are, indeed, a quick learner, as your other mentors have suggested."

"Where do you think Shadi will go next?" Ajmal scanned the edges of rocks again for his former mentor.

"Where he pleases. He may have liked you, but be aware you were also a burden."

"I tried not to be."

"That is good. I meant no insult. Shadi would possibly take you back with him, but he understands your place is not here."

"Perterra is all I have ever known. Why should I leave?"

"There are many ways of knowing. As to why you should leave is a matter for you to discover very soon. I will give you only one hint: you were never meant to be here. It is all of us who have adjusted to your presence until such time as you are able to return to the dominion of men."

Within a short time, Faraj and Ajmal discussed Aristotle and Socrates before sliding in human history to more recent philosophers and thinkers, agreeing on aspects of Hegel's ideas but arguing over interpretations of Foucault's work.

"We are unlikely to agree on Nietzsche's theories either," said Ajmal, tossing a stick into the wind. As they spoke, the piece of wood continued to sail further and further away until it could not be seen. "I understand the rules of gravity are different here in Perterra," mused Ajmal more to himself than to Faraj. "How will I get used to being so heavily tied to Earth when all I have known is Perterra?"

"We are also affected by gravity here but with much less force than in your world. It is why you can leap so high. Now, let's take a metaphorical leap. Back to philosophy. Friedrich Nietzsche didn't agree with Friedrich Nietzsche's writings if you compare his later work to that of the younger philosopher," offered Faraj.

"Was he mad at the end or revealing himself as a confused old man, demented maybe?" asked Ajmal.

"Everything is revealing, even when intended to disguise," said Faraj.

"The Übermensch?"

"What do you think? I don't want your repetitions of his ideas but your own analysis now."

"I think that I would not have been cast out if such superior men existed. I believe men are inferior in whole and in part. I, too, by my very biology, am inferior to all of you in Perterra, even you, the least of my mentors."

"Least? Still concerned with size, I see. And why am I least, as you say? Perhaps, after a time, you will be a better judge of my abilities and your own. Men, they are a most difficult species if we are going to consider concepts of superiority. Perhaps such superior women exist."

Ajmal smiled then wrinkled his forehead. "What happened to my mother? Why did she leave me? If you know as much as you claim, you should be able to give me answers that are not riddles or dead ends."

"Again, with these questions I cannot answer," said Faraj.

"I will keep asking. You see, I am past being worried about annoying my mentors if I want to discover something. I just want to know if the woman threw me away or something happened to her. Is she still alive as has been suggested?"

Faraj said nothing but moved along, sliding through tall grasses, making it hard at moments for Ajmal to spot him.

"Have I annoyed you again?" asked Ajmal.

Faraj slowly wound his way out of the grasses and over the sand. Ajmal followed the serpentine motions of the snake which made patterns in the dunes. Turning, Ajmal looked at the lines they had drawn and thought the pattern might be read. At first, lines were too blurred, then the separation became recognizable.

"Look at our tracks," Ajmal said. "Yours and mine. What do you think our writing says about us?" he asked.

Catching the boy's tone, Faraj said, "You should not jest. Our lines reveal a great deal. Look again, only this time with greater care."

As Ajmal studied the curves and contours of their demarcations in the sand, he saw that the lines began apart then converged, moved apart again, then together. "We are walking the same path in life," he said, "even when we seem to be diverging."

"We are as one, but only for now. Soon, your direction will veer away from mine. Then we will know it is time for you to make your last journey from here."

"I do not want to leave my friends—all I have ever known. I'm sorry if I have been rude or offended you in some way. That, too, is my curse."

"Don't be sorry. It is your nature to be generous and thoughtful, but there is a reason you came to us and a reason you have learned so much. I, myself, would not want to leave Perterra for that other realm either."

"What if I do the wrong thing when I somehow get back?"

"What do you do if you make a mistake here in Perterra?"

"Try to correct it and go forward."

"There. You have your answer without my help at all."

"And my mother?"

"Look at the tracks again."

"We are on the same path?"

"You cannot see a snake smile, but I am smiling."

XI

Naimah Speaks About Peace

In New York, Naimah opened the window curtain ever so slightly and looked out. It had begun to snow—crystalline shapes the size of silver coins, and she thought she had never seen the sky release such beauty. Writing the first words in her new book, her fingers froze, catching the pen in mid-motion. Calming her inclination and closing her eyes, she allowed pen to follow its own course, walking at first then dancing across the page. Learning English, she played with syntax rather than simply inflection as she would have in Arabic, the import of the word finding its position in the statement. When she had written several pages, she grew restless, and decided to leave her small space.

Walking out at night, Naimah slowed her pace behind a woman talking angrily and loudly on her cell phone. "You'll never amount to anything," said the woman into her phone. "I've wasted too much money on you and for what? For what? You've done nothing but disappoint me," the stranger yelled at an absent son. "What kind of a son are you? What have you become?"

Naimah walked past the woman, then turned. "It is not my place to say anything to you, but be glad you have a son; be happy he is alive."

"What?" The angry woman calmed and looked instantly guilt-ridden.

"Your son is alive. I am happy for you both," Naimah said.

Turning away again, Naimah could hear the woman sigh then tell her son, "All right. All right. I got a little carried away. I'm sorry, too. Yes, some crazy woman in the street was talking. What were you saying again?"

Naimah waited for the light at the cross walk and hurried on her way. Although she could not hear the rest of their conversation, she felt a little relief that the mother and son were still talking. She wondered if she would have argued with a grown Ajmal.

*

The audience seemed like an enemy when she walked out on stage, a spotlight already trained on her like soldier's fire. Naimah could feel sweat beading up on her forehead and on the back of her neck. Looking out over the sea of heads dimly lit, Naimah swallowed hard. The first time she spoke in front of an audience, her voice caught half-way up her throat, and Naimah thought she would die on that auditorium stage, choking on her own words. Discomfort of those waiting felt like a thistle on her tongue. Time swept up into a ball in which she had no idea how long she had been standing there in a menacing room.

Then she remembered her baby the night before they fled, and she found her strength again. "Good evening. I am here tonight to tell you a simple story." A velvet voice emerged, wrapping around the women and men in attendance until all were struggling to reign in their closely held emotions. She wove a fable in which men and women lived together in peace, but then she told her audience that her tale was not a lie but only a dream. That they were the ones who could make the peace real. After a silence, they applauded her words.

*

Her manuscript with its exquisite illustrations crossed an editor's desk on the right day. What Naimah did not know was her success was as dependent on luck as her sorrows. Margaret, the woman who would become Naimah's editor, had grown weary of cynicism crossing her purview all day and was concerned about her own son's descent into first drugs and then homelessness. Phillip had schizophrenia which had gone undiagnosed for too long, and he had used drugs to self-medicate. Margaret was momentarily fragile in the instant she picked up Naimah's pages, mailed to her by Naimah's college professor. It was circumstance and sorrow rather than connections or talent alone that caused Margaret to push for publication of the work of this unknown Muslim woman who had fled a war-torn Middle Eastern country. A woman who had lost her son, like me, Margaret thought.

When Margaret called Naimah, the editor was excited but full of advice: "Too many animals, reduce the number of characters, and increase their impact, and for God's sake, create a happier ending. No one wants to read about an unresolved, endless search." Even as she said those words, the editor thought of her son, her vulnerability still pushed below surface.

"Even if what is unresolved is the truth?"

"Especially because that sadness is closer to truth. And you need a better title. Jazz it up a little."

Naimah considered her simple title and struggled with a change. She read some titles in magazines at the library: "Murder Crawling in the Open Window," "Sleight of Hand in a New York Winter."

She talked to her professor at the city college. "I don't think I can change the title. It must be my son's name. How will he ever find me?"

Her professor looked amused for a moment then serious. "Why is a title change so important? Listen to your editor and change it if that will help you get the story published. I don't think you have any idea how fortunate you are that someone is looking at your work. I've been trying to get a top tier editor to look at my manuscript for years." Hunching his shoulders, he instantly regretted inserting his own ambitions into the conversation with his student.

"Perhaps my son will somehow know his name and find me. That is why I must keep this title. I would not be searching if I had never lost my son; I would not have written this book."

"After all this time, you are still searching, believing he is alive?" the professor was truly surprised and felt guilty he had questioned her and inserted his own insecurities. "I suppose you have considered the impossibility of this line of thought?"

"I do not know what is possible or impossible, but I'd rather go on searching than forget."

"Then let your title speak for itself. Fight for the name. Some things are worth the risk."

*

Writing became Naimah's path to making sense of the changes in her life, still viewed as a violent, cruel expanse where a baby could be lost to his injured mother, and orphans could be made every minute of every day in man's endless wars. Inside the pages of worn books tossed away by others, she wrote her stories, her words winding around another's, dipping below margins, so that one story was told inside another.

She tried reimagining what had happened the night she was struck down: a piece of shrapnel from an explosion hit a rock in the road then glanced off her forehead. Fortunately, it was not a killing blow because the strike was not direct. Her wound, however, was deep, and she was knocked unconscious. The doctors told her that she had been unresponsive for several days before suddenly awakening to terror. Her baby was gone! Putting down her pen, she struggled with writing that scene. What she was told meant nothing to what she felt.

Outside, fighting dogs yelped in the alley below. They lunged and barked, cried and begged for a scrap left in the streets, bloodying one another until a smaller dog, long ago scarred, gave in and ran off, barking in a high pitch whine like a child. Naimah recognized the yelp as pain. Perhaps she would write about hungry dogs, too.

*

There were critics at every turn, Naimah thought. As soon as her book was released, it seemed to make some people angry.

"How dare she write a book when she has no credentials, no position from which to claim authority," said another city college English professor, who wrote a letter to Naimah's editor. He had never met Naimah and assumed she had gotten published through some devious means, his own manuscript languishing in a drawer, he suggested at the end of the missive.

"I am an only authority on losing my son, and that is what I have written," she wanted to tell him.

She could hear his derisive laughter in the manner of his words that cut like fine knives: "The author feigns humility, but it is the height of arrogance to think she can change anything, alter a single perspective on the absurdity of creating peace," he wrote. "Man is inclined and intended to be violent. Violence is also our means of survival." Her editor read the words again as if unsure of their meaning before she laughed derisively.

Naimah wanted to respond to him: "It would appear arrogant that you feel compelled to belittle me and my efforts not meant to harm. But please, take no offense. More than anything, my story is longing." She did not write to him, however, or argue with Margaret about why her editor read her the cruel remarks in the first place.

Naimah did ask her editor, however, why? "Why did you want me to hear his words?"

"I simply wanted to demonstrate the foolishness that I have to deal with all the time," said Margaret as she tossed her hair's curls and threw a dried-out pen away, creating an echoing rattle. "I don't really expect you to read all their criticisms," Margaret said, already feeling guilty. "If they are writing anything about your book, it is good for you, regardless of the comments. At least, it means someone has noticed. The more notice—of any kind—the better."

*

Naimah wanted to follow the editor's advice, but she found herself reading the next comment that appeared as a review of her work. "This little, graphic novella reeks of sentimentality. Any realistic presentation precludes survival of the son, and how absurd to think a poor, ignorant Middle Eastern woman would write a book in English, no less, let alone land a book contract in NYC. Good God! The plot, wording, the arbitrariness of it all are preposterous. This is nothing more than a fable."

"Ah, but you did write a book," said Margaret pleased with herself.

"And I had it published!"

"Thank you," said Naimah. "Why was this reader so angry?"

"Stop paying attention to all these negatives. We call them trolls. By the way, I have another speaking engagement lined up for you." Margaret pulled out her phone calendar and read the date.

"I only have my little stories."

"Your little stories have incredible power. Keep writing them. The more you speak, the more people will want to read your words."

What else could I do? Naimah wondered as she left her editor's office, thinking about her stories reaching out like tentacles, so far that even a lost boy might hear them. Ah, no, she thought, he would be a young man now.

XII

Edge of Perterra

Saleh, the great black horse, strode up to Ajmal, lowering his magnificent head with long mane. Ajmal reached his hand out and stoked the stallion's narrow face. They instantly liked one another.

"You will take him the rest of the way," said Faraj. "But first, this boy must rest. We have journeyed a long way together without the benefit of your strong legs."

"Will you miss me?" Ajmal asked of Faraj. "I knew with the others, but you have been harder to read."

"Then I have taught you well."

"That is your answer?"

"Snakes are never very cuddly creatures, even in Perterra," said Faraj, "but if you must know, you will be missed." He wound around Ajmal's left leg before loosening himself again.

Ajmal smiled. "I will miss you, too. Does that surprise you?"

"Not at all. You are more transparent than you suspect. Now, I have to greet my old friend Salah and will say good-bye." Faraj slithered around some dry brush before disappearing.

"Good-bye, Faraj," Ajmal said, then added, "my friend." He built and stoked a small fire then sat down and curled up next to it, listening to Saleh discuss his journeys for a few minutes before drifting off to sleep.

As Ajmal dreamed, he heard Saleh say, "Are you telling me this young man could possibly make a difference in their violent, chaotic sphere? What power does he have? Without us, he would long ago have perished here, as well as in their fractured lands."

"He has the great power to inspire love," said Faraj. "Look how we have set everything aside for him, as his mother once did. I had absolutely no intention of growing fond of him, and yet I have."

"He must be very powerful then. Perhaps he will change them."

"I suspect it is not the boy who will change their world," said Faraj. "It will be his mother, but he will play an important part. He is needed in some way we do not yet understand."

*

In the morning, Ajmal stretched then got up to prepare a meal. Looking around for Faraj, Ajmal already knew that his mentor had gone before asking the question.

"You must ride now," said Saleh. "Don't fear. We will get along well, and I am strong enough to carry you across all the wide lands of Perterra."

"Where are we going?"

"It is not a physical destination but a state of mind."

The teen climbed on the back of the great horse, holding the mane. "How will I know when we are there then?" he spoke near the horse's long ear that twitched with his warming whisper.

"I will carry you to lands you have never seen, to the ends of Perterra, and in that place you will seek the one for whom you are searching."

"Am I to look for my mother then?"

"None other."

*

Their ride lasted over a year. Saleh carried Ajmal through wind and storms, never stumbling. As the boy rode, he talked, and Saleh answered haltingly, often out of breath.

"I do not wish to complain, but I am tired of riding."

"And I am tired of carrying you," said Saleh, "but if I have the stamina to carry you so far, you must have the strength merely to ride."

"Riding is not always easy as you imagine. I must constantly adjust and cannot sleep while you leap and race below me. My legs are sore."

"Have we so thoroughly spoiled you, boy?"

"Not at all. I'm simply making an observation. And I'm no longer a boy."

"Here is my observation. You're not being compassionate. Baltasar carried you when you were a child and very light. I must shoulder you when you are nearly a man."

"You think I'm nearly a man, then?"

"By the size of you alone."

"I'm sorry, but your conversation is not as stimulating as my previous teachers," Ajmal said in a moment of weakness, wishing to convey his annoyance at the dismissal of his aches.

"And you are heavier than any I have ever carried," said Saleh. "Fortunately for us both, we have arrived at a place where you can make your camp."

Dismounting, the young man read the books left to him where man and horse bedded for the night.

"Your education must continue."

"When will I know enough to reenter their dimension?"

"You must read and learn for the rest of your days. Your education is never over," said Saleh as he pawed the ground out of restless exhaustion.

"Why never? I'm no longer a child, as you said. Please don't treat me like one now."

"I treat you as I wish to be treated—honestly. Learning is for men as well as boys. When you stop learning and reading, you will grow dull and disappear. But your biology demands you eat first. Then study."

First looking back at the campfire, Ajmal set about preparations for a meal of finely ground corn, perfecting the mush and setting it on a stone plate. He felt he had never tasted better food. Saleh grazed on the tall grasses nearby, and for a while the only sound was the man and horse moving their teeth and tongues.

"What will it feel like when I return?"

"I don't really know."

"I thought my teachers knew everything."

"Then you are indeed foolish."

"Sorry. I meant that it would seem you might have an idea to help me."

"It may feel horrible at first. You will wish to turn back, but there is no reentrance to Perterra for you."

"Never? Even if I want to come back? You will not have me?"

Saleh shook his head, and his long mane looked like a river moving in two directions. "I would have you stay as friend forever but have no say in the matter. Neither do you. It is simply your time soon. Just as it was not your choice to enter Perterra, it will not be a choice to return. You will have one more guide before your abrupt re-entrance, however. We must all make the best of our circumstances whatever they may be."

"Was I really a terrible burden?"

"Of course, but one I grew to love." Saleh was silent. After several moments, Ajmal asked him another question but heard no response. Saleh fell asleep standing, and Ajmal knew the stallion was already dreaming as his nostrils twitched.

"You have come far with me and never asked for anything in return. I thank you." Ajmal rubbed the great horse's neck. Saleh stirred but did not wake. With his mentors, Ajmal had always been fearless, but now doubt crept into him, thinking of man's domain. Yet, despite his nervous fears, Ajmal slept more soundly than he had in a very long time. Something was settled in him. He knew he was returning to the realm of men and would not fight leaving Perterra. He would finally meet his mother.

77

*

In the morning, Saleh nudged Ajmal awake. "I must go now."

"What? Already?"

"We have arrived at the place you will meet your last mentor in Perterra. Yahla is much faster and cleverer than me."

Ajmal took Saleh's mane in his fist and held it tight. "I don't wish you to go."

"This is hard for me, as well, but in the end, it will be better if I go quickly. Yahla is already here in the low grasses." Saleh shook his mane to free the young man's hand, then he raced up a slope and disappeared over the hill.

Ajmal looked around terrified for an instant before recalling his training and the firm echoes of his guides. When a dragonfly lit on a rock near him, Ajmal reached out, allowing the insect to lite on his upturned palm. "Yahla?" He thought for an instant that the insect was to be his next mentor, but that did not turn out to be the case.

The insect said nothing to him. Was this how insects would act in that other sphere? The dragonfly seemed unable to speak or read or instruct Ajmal, yet Ajmal felt comforted by its mere presence and intuited he would be able to manage in the large, loud construct men inhabited.

XIII

Naimah Considers Newton's Mountain

Only after reading extensively did Naimah discover wonder then anger that she had once been denied an education by those who loved her. She read about "war capitalism" and came to recognize how players on another continent could induce wars in her own country. War for profit: those who made war for gains in a paroxysm of greed were removed physically from the immediacy and horror but not from the moral and ethical weight of lost children. Peace would not arrive through prayer but some other means, if at all.

Writing day and night, Naimah theorized that if Newton could postulate about gravitational pull, later realized with man's satellites, she could write her own thought experiment about peace. If a story were to compel enough people that they ceased fighting for any length of time, then peace could be achieved on one bit of soil, spreading far. If she could conceive of it, others could, too.

Naimah had earlier attended a class and learned about the great mathematician/scientist Newton and his Laws of Motion. It was the theory of the cannon on the mountain which stayed with her. She did not love the science but the analogy and visualizing the thought experiment, as it was called.

"Your idea for a story is a dream only a woman would have," said Sanders, an adjunct instructor at the community college she was attending. "Man will never be able to have peace. It is in his nature to be warring and violent, to clash with other cultures and within his own."

"But a woman might," said Naimah, simply, without arrogance.

"Only a woman would say such a ridiculous thing. Man is used generically here. That which cannot be achieved might still be imagined is worth nothing."

"Ah, only a woman or a man such as Newton or Einstein or Picasso or Shakespeare could imagine," she said smiling.

"You prove what, exactly? Imagination is futility. None you have mentioned; you have only demonstrated that your totems are men."

"Which is why we have not had lasting peace. Perhaps a woman—Newton could not prove his 'thought experiment,' but he could envision it. Only many years later, could we see that a metal object moving at a certain rate would continue to orbit rather than fall. Our satellites, you see. Newton was correct although he could not prove it at the time."

"There is a difference between science and your infantile, wishful thinking in the form of childish social comment: 'There is a distant rumble.'"

"But what follows is choice," Naimah protested.

"Wars are never far behind. That is the demonstrated choice human kind has made."

"If we move at the same speed away from wars as they move toward us, then—"

"It is industry, not war you hear echoes of. Is your diatribe against man, or wars, or the entire industrial complex of the West?"

"War is not inevitable. We write, we listen, we reason. But if we do nothing to stop the erosion of land, as well as reason, well, then we must accept war. But…even the flying insects are dying, biomass loss. Earth has lost a third of her land. When the land is no longer arable, the people migrate toward the cities, and the crush, that disturbance of balance pushes us all further toward extinction. There is an interconnection between the industry of man and his wars."

"I will not continue to argue with you. I understand things will end badly, but your premise for a book, a fable, really, is silly."

"Without cynicism."

"Without reason, as women so often are wont to do."

"Virginia Woolf," Naimah said, turning once before leaving the professor. She thought about his need to belittle her. She wished she had said, "I see a distant shore where no landmass can be, and I know we have other, seldom used other senses." She did not know from where this image came.

Naimah ended her book in discomfort and doubt but no longer sorrow. Peace would remain elusive and tenuous but it was her goal to work for it. She had released her fierce hold on anger and grief but hope still hung about her. Some mornings, she watched hope slide along surfaces and into cracks, but then it would suddenly appear along the window sill with a slant of sunlight. She called it out again, rooms sometimes as unforgiving as man's history.

*

"Make it a happy ending," her editor had said, several, large rings on her bony long fingers sliding with the play of her thumb.

"But it would not be true."

"Oh, truth is vastly overrated. We all need a little fantasy to survive." The editor's son had not called her in three months. She was no longer certain he was alive.

"It has been too many years for a happy ending." Naimah said.

"Well, then, at least don't dismiss the possibility of a reunion. We all need something to hang onto, just as you do."

"I would never dismiss that possibility. There is something I must tell you, Margaret."

"Yes, what is it? Don't keep me in suspense."
"I am going blind."
"What? Have you been to a doctor? Maybe you need glasses."
"Macular degeneration. It is fairly slow. I have some time yet."
"Oh, my god, Naimah. What will you do?"
"I accept what must be. I thought you should know."
"I refuse to accept that bleak diagnosis. Let me give you a name of an ophthalmologist."
"Thank you."
"What are you going to do?"
"Work quickly. I still have some time."
"Oh, Naimah, there is never enough time."

*

Many months before, Naimah had written to her cousin Raafe, hoping to tell him where she was living and offer to give him a home in America. She feared they would never reconnect with the wars, lost homes, and broken communications. He and her aunt were her only family left.

When she went down to her mailbox in the lobby of her apartment building, she jumped back after taking out an envelope. It was a letter from Raafe. He was weary but alive.

"No, I will not come to America, the oppressor," he wrote. "But I will wish you well and a long life. I must continue to take care of my ailing mother who sends her love." In his last line, he wrote the words that stayed with Naimah: "I have never stopped searching for your son. For an instant, I imagine seeing him in the eyes of orphans and angry boys. I recognize him in my brothers-in-arms. But I have yet to discover your Ajmal, the boy with the blue birthmark and the kind mother."

Naimah sat on the cold floor in the alcove with the many mailboxes and wept.

XIV

Leaving Perterra

Like a water color painting, shapes around Ajmal blurred, and definition became a stroke elongated past intention, another cut short by bleeding rains. There was no map leading to or out of Perterra, no certain path or longitudinal direction.

He knelt near a patch of blue light and followed water lines with his eyes.

"What should I do?" he asked his last companion Yahya, a sleek cheetah, as he climbed atop moss-covered rocks.

"Seek your own kind. You must find yourself again and look for your mother. We have gone as far as we can go with you." Yahya licked his paw, first one then the other, being a clean cat.

"My mentors have taught me much, but I still don't know what to look for. How could I find the world of men? How could I possibly find my mother, if she is even alive?"

"Begin again by listening."

"My mother would be an old woman by now. How would I recognize her?"

"She will not be old, just wiser," said Yahya. "Remember, you accepted us as your guides without any evidence whatsoever that we would not harm you. You listened to your instincts then. Sometimes, you must listen with your soul instead of your intellect. Both will serve you well in your next journey."

Ajmal was frustrated with the vagueness of his mentor. He stomped his foot as if an angry horse. "I won't know how. Their dominion is too bright and noisy. I could hear it in my dreams one morning."

Yahya was not bothered by the young man's impatience and annoyance. Rather, he answered his questions as truthfully as he was able. "That is the thinning. It means you are ready. At first, living in their world will be hard. You must adjust to the harsher quality of light and sound."

"Already the land is changing color," he said, noticing the red outcropping and burnt umber soil. "I have been gone from there a long time. I have no memory of it," the young man said to his companion. "I'm not so sure, I'll be able to adjust."

"Then you will live on your own terms without adjustment, but you must go back." Yahya was stealthily moving further away.

A loud booming noise startled Ajmal. "Is it their war?"

"Not yet. Only a construction barge and crane, repairing damage. But that is their world you hear. We are very near. I can feel as well as hear them, too." Another boulder was dropped from the crane and echoed in their ears. "Perterra is disappearing for you. It is natural, but you must hurry. Perhaps there will be a way for you to find yourself there and to find your mother."

"Where will I find you? How will I get back to Baltasar and Saleh and Faraj?"

"Don't look for us."

"This is a terrible place I must enter. I decided I don't want to go there."

"Oh, no, not at all, not a terrible place. Just vastly different. Find what is good in man's world, my young friend. There is so much more to them than war."

"Where will I come out? What country will I be in? Which of their crazy languages must I speak?"

"It is arranged for you to be near the point your mother is living."

"How arranged? I don't understand. If you could do this, why did you wait all these years before making me go back?"

"It is our hope you will be able to more readily find her," said Yahya without addressing the young man's accusations.

"But, I'm sorry, I don't even know what she looks like. Tell me about her again. Please, if you know."

"She looks like you. Don't be afraid. Trust your instincts. You know she is called Naimah, and she is going blind."

"Blind? What can I do? How is this supposed to help me?"

"Her impending blindness will not help you; you are to help her. It is why you must return now. Your mother is a writer. Without her eyes, her books promoting peace may not be written or find their readers."

"Why tell me this? There is nothing I can do. We are as foreign as enemies."

"No, you are as close as wind and water. Soon, you will be with her, and you could be her eyes. You will be her hands as she dictates. You may one day become her voice and the voice of reason to the unreasoning."

Over his head, Ajmal noticed a great bird he had never seen before, soaring, stretching wide wings across horizon. Ajmal could not have identified the osprey as he had never come across one in Perterra.

"Is that a bird of Perterra or from the other realm?"

"Your world, now, my young friend, but I must go because the thinning is here."

Ajmal reached his hand out to touch the soft fur of Yahya's head, the cheetah bending low. "Come with me," he whispered.

"You know I cannot exist under their dominion."

"There are cheetahs there. I've seen pictures of cheetahs in books."

"Not like me, I'm afraid, but perhaps you will find comfort in those animals. Good-bye, Ajmal. You are a man now. Don't forget me."

"Yahla," said Ajmal as his mentor raced over lands into the blue.

Ajmal turned to look up at the disappearing osprey again before scanning the horizon once more for Yahya. In his place, a pine had taken shape. The spine of the tree was somehow familiar, not as memory but as knowledge he had acquired through reading. As he looked around, colors changed, and shadows slipped away. Without analysis, he understood he had passed into the realm of men. The half-awoken morning was red with warning, but he could not retreat from where he had entered.

He took a deep breath and listened as the decibels of human activity rushed in, startling. Somehow, his animal mentors had brought him the length and breadth of Perterra and delivered him to the world. They had known all along, he realized. They were simply waiting for him to be ready to make the crossing, and he had done it without conscious decision.

Emerging as if a newborn but, this time, Ajmal was imbued with knowledge and history and sorrow. He did not remember the loss of his mother, but he keenly knew the loss of his mentors and friends.

XV

Marketing, Branding, and the Selling of a Promise

A successful book is one simply that is read and appreciated by someone in addition to the author, Naimah told her editor.

"I'm afraid not, my dear Naimah. A successful book is one that sells and brings in loads of money for the publisher and, occasionally a little for the author."

Naimah believed her book would open another's eyes, but she didn't know if it would sell well. "But if I change one person's mind," she said, thinking that reader would be someone who could see more than violence and understand how wars altered all of their lives.

"Don't worry so much," said Margaret. Her editor added that Naimah's graphic novel was selling well enough for her to earn her first, small royalty check. "I know it's not enough to live on yet, but you must keep writing."

"I am doing okay," said Naimah who had found work as a receptionist at her city college. She did not tell Margaret that the royalty checks she earned were the most money she had ever seen at once.

"You have a reading coming up. Successful authors are the ones who are willing to put in the time and effort to market along with the publisher. We are partners in this venture, remember."

"Yet, so little time to write," sighed Naimah.

Margaret felt guilty but congratulated herself on getting Naimah's thin book past the other editors who didn't think an illustrated, anti-war book was sexy enough to take a risk on publishing.

"At least market it as a graphic novel not a fable," said Graydon, another editor. Margaret told Naimah they would call the story a graphic novel. "The illustrations are beautiful."

"I understand, naming is important. Your son?" asked Naimah. "Have you heard anything from him yet?" She knew her connection to Margaret was strengthened by their losses as much as by their meager success.

"Nothing. But the reality is, if he was dead, I think I would know. I will take silence as hopeful as you have told me on more than one occasion."

"Yes. Perhaps he will again reach out to you."

"Ever the optimist. Of course, that is what I love about you."

Naimah did not think of herself as an optimistic person at all.

"Are you ready for your reading? People like to have the author present before buying. It is getting harder and harder to sell books, you know. Truth be told, we're in a dying industry. Too few readers, too many writers."

This was something Naimah could not understand, books having made her long and difficult journey over the years more bearable, given her purpose and comfort, distracted her when she felt at her lowest. "I understand and appreciate everything you have done for me. I am ready."

"I'm trying to line up a speaker's bureau for you. Once you're on the speaker circuit, promotions will be easier. Your audience will grow. We just have to create a brand for you."

"A brand?"

"It's just a marketing expression, meaning we have to package you and your ideas."

"Oh, I don't think I wish to be packaged."

"I promise, it won't hurt at all. It will be good to have more people read your book. Maybe they will think about war differently—not about winning or losing but from the perspective of all the victims, all those hurt and killed in wars."

"That is more than I could ask for."

"Well, we can be ambitious and hope for fame and money rewards, too, can't we?"

Naimah didn't tell her editor that she was not writing for fame or out of ambition. "I hope you hear from your son soon."

XVI

Ajmal Finds a Brother

Traveling on foot, then catching a ride with a stranger, Ajmal road in a car into the city. The man who stopped surprised him, but they talked very little.

"You look like you're a long way from home," the young man driving the car said.

"Very, very far. Thank you for stopping."

"Heading into the city?"

"Yes." Ajmal hesitated before asking, "What city?"

The driver laughed. "You're kidding right? Only the greatest city on Earth and a couple other planets. New York, the Big Apple, the City that Never Sleeps."

"She must be very tired," said Ajmal.

Again, the driver laughed. "Listen, kid, your jokes are a little lame. Better work on them before you try out your routine in a night club."

"They will get better," said Ajmal.

The car was sleek and shiny, faster than all of Ajmal's animal mentors. Perhaps this world offered something more he would love. The language and dress of the driver had already told Ajmal he had landed in America. He wondered how he would ever find his mother or his way in this city of millions.

*

"Hey, good luck," said the driver.

"Thank you for your generosity and kindness. You, too, should have good fortune," said Ajmal, climbing out.

"Listen, kid, don't talk to everybody that way," said the driver, leaning out his open window. "I mean, be a little nastier, okay? Hate to see you eaten up your first day." He shot his hand up in a wave.

"Okay," Ajmal said, repeating the driver's gesture. "Eaten?"

*

With his clever tongue and sharp mind, Ajmal found a job working as a dishwasher in a restaurant, after following the "Help Wanted" sign in the window. The manager let him sleep in the basement of the building for half his wages. In time, Ajmal would find the lay of the city and other opportunities. Many around him spoke English, but some spoke multiple other languages, all of which Ajmal was comfortable around. He knew he had landed far from the place of his birth.

"How come you can speak so many languages?" asked Jose as they shoved their raw, red hands into scalding hot water with dishes.

"It is part of my teaching."

"What kind of school is that?"

"A school in which everything and everyone is there to help you learn."

"I wish I'd had a school like that. You talk kind of funny, too. Like you're educated, so what are you doing washing dishes?"

"It is a fine job. See what good conversations we have."

"You're weird all right but a good kind of strange."

"Maybe you can help me to navigate the city."

"I only know this neighborhood, but it's not that hard. Just hop on the train, that's the subway, okay. Listen, you gotta learn slang, city slang. There's plenty of foreigners here with every kind of accent, but you can't go around sounding like you just stepped out of a time warp."

"Ah, I see. Maybe I did."

Jose looked hard at Ajmal for a moment then laughed. "You know, you're kind of funny, too."

"You will teach me slang?"

"Sure thing. Let's start with basics. If some dude walks up to you and puts out his chest and says, 'let's take it outside,' you walk away. It means he wants to fight you, and you don't look like a fighter to me."

"I am more than capable of defending myself."

"Well, to be on the side of caution—you not about that life. And if somebody says you or they acting all 'thirsty,' it don't mean they want a drink. Means they desperate."

"Thank you. I will remember."

"Now, don't be thanking people for this or anything. There's the word 'guap' which means money, so don't be trying to get them some guacamole or something. If you want to show you telling truth, you say, 'dead ass, B.'"

"I can see I have a great deal to learn."

"That's 'kay. You my son."

"Your son? I'm afraid I don't—"

"See, right there. 'Son' is a friend but don't be too casual 'bout it."

"Then you are my son, too," said Ajmal. Jose laughed again.

"Hey, we gotta get you some ice after you get paid."

"Ice?"

"Chains, bling for your neck, you know."

"Then I will look like I belong?"

"Yeah, as long as you don't open your mouth first."

The two young men worked silently, then raced to see which one could clean the greatest number of dishes and glasses without breakage.

*

Remembering his anthropomorphic guides in Perterra and their advice to find the city's greatest number of books, Ajmal took the subway to a stop near the New York City Public Library. The imposing lions at the steps met him, and Ajmal half expected them to speak to him, but they remained silent. It was time he found some new books. Running up the steps with his new chain bouncing against his neck and on his chest, he stopped inside the massive doors. There, on the wall, was a poster announcing an author's reading at a nearby bookstore. Her name was Naimah. "Listen to your instincts," Yahya had told him. How could it be his mother, yet Ajmal knew he must attend this reading.

XVII

Unfamiliar Familiar

The evening before her reading and book signing, Naimah had a dream. Waking in fear and confusion, she vividly recalled the disorienting scene. She had been standing in a dark room looking out through a tall screen door to a lake which was unfamiliar. Even in dreaming, she heard the rain beating the roof, porch, walls around her. Everything was weeping. Sounds of water falling in a sudden rush caused her to turn her head away. When she looked back out through the screen, a man's figure stood on the other side. He did not speak or move, but Naimah knew. This was her grown son Ajmal. He had come to her but could not cross that threshold. Then she sat up in the bed, shaking.

*

While Naimah was signing her books at a corner table in a bookstore, thinking about how to personalize each statement with her signature, an older woman came up to the table. "Could you tell me how to publish my book?"

Naimah shook her head but gave her a card with her editor's name. "It is difficult," she offered, "but do not give up."

"You can't imagine how many places I've already tried. How about your publisher? Could you mention my book? Here's my card with the book tile. It's a memoir about my father and me."

Naimah took the woman's card and set it in her bag. The woman left without purchasing Naimah's book she left open on the table.

Sitting there for an hour and selling only four books during that time, Naimah was not discouraged. There were always amusing and strange interactions with those who came to talk but not buy. Other authors would stop and ask about her publishing experiences. It seemed as if every person who stopped by was another writer.

Until one woman asked where Naimah was from and if she was a legal immigrant or "one of those illegals." Thin veneers wore off quickly with bigoted remarks, but Naimah had long practiced patience and kindness, so these intrusions were only sleights.

"Guess you came to America to get rich off us," said a tall blond woman, still hovering.

"No. I simply want to live and write."

"Nothing simple about living here. I hope you realize how lucky you are. And, you had better stay out of trouble or they'll deport you," the woman remarked, eyeing her suspiciously before walking away.

An elderly man asked if she was currently dating anyone. "I've never dated a Muslim woman before, but I could," he said with a smile, winking at her. Naimah shook her head but was polite. "Guess that's a no, then?"

"I'm sorry, but you are correct."

"Not my lucky day," he said. "I'm not much to look at, but I could show you a good time."

Naimah shook her head, and the man wandering off to look for another woman alone in the store.

Waiting quietly as she had done all of her life, Naimah opened the pages of her book and reread a sentence. If she was going to advocate for peace, she knew she must work at engaging people in conversation. It was hard. What they wanted from her seemed far from what she had to offer. They did not want to talk about her book or why she wrote. They did not ask her what happened to her son or if she ever found him. They did not even broach the subject of her search. Even with a lifetime of enduring and honing her acceptance of others, she was growing not weary but angry. Anger would not help, she knew. She had pushed it back down many times. It would only turn those away who might someday be persuaded to enter into asking for peace. She took a sip of water and returned to autographing copies she would leave in the store.

*

When a young man's voice asked her to sign a book, she did not look up at first. He studied the way she held the pen before Naimah turned her stare to him. He sensed a familiarity immediately. There was no need to ask his mentors for assistance or to question them about his instincts. With her book in the long, slender fingers of one hand, he reached out with the other and touched her wrist. The beating of his heart followed the cadence in her pulse. "Please," he said, as if asking permission to touch her.

She was not embarrassed but startled. He let her go as if in shock. For several seconds, they stared at each other. Naimah's eyes adjusted to the altered light as she studied his face, wishing to touch it.

"Would you sign something for me?" he asked.

Still puzzled by the young man's intimate tone, Naimah asked, "What would you like me to write?"

"You lost a son," said Ajmal. "I lost a mother. Your book," said her son. "What you have written and have yet to write will be very important. You must keep working and speaking about peace. I'm sorry if I sound too bold in this moment, but I wish to help you to get your message out to others. I will become your eyes."

"My eyes? How could you know? It is not possible." One stroke of astonishment after another landed on her, but the blows were gentle like evening's wind in summer.

Quite suddenly, the young man changed aspect. "Yes, it is possible. All of it." he said, encouraging her to discover the place at which he had already arrived.

Then, she saw her father in the young man's wide forehead and small ears pressed close to his head. In the long face were the strong bones of her husband's jawline. But his eyes, now welling with tears, his eyes were all his own. And in the corner of his left eye, there was a tiny blue birthmark.

"Ajmal, my son, oh, my beautiful son," she said, opening her arms.

Additional published works by **Nancy A. Dafoe** include the Vena Goodwin murder mystery series of novels: *You Enter A Room, Both End in Speculation,* and *Murder on Ponte Vecchio.*

Dafoe's poetry books include *Poets Diving in the Night* and *Innermost Sea,* containing the William Faulkner/William Wisdom award winning poem "Entrance Exam."

Her books on education consist of a policy book, *The Misdirection of Education Policy,* and two writing instruction books, *Breaking Open the Box* and *Writing Creatively.*

Dafoe's memoir *An Iceberg in Paradise: A Passage Through Alzheimer's* was published in 2015.

Her fiction and nonfiction work also appears in several anthologies, including *Lost Orchard* and *Lost Orchard II,* as well as *NY Votes for Women: A Suffrage Centennial Anthology.*

In addition to her work appearing in various journals, Dafoe's writing may be found on her three blog sites online through Dafoe Writing and Consulting, Nancy Dafoe Books, and the Indivisible Cortland County website, and A Place for Mom website dealing with Alzheimer's care.

Dafoe has given workshops on writing at various locations including the Downtown Writers Center in Syracuse, NY and the Center for the Arts in Homer, NY. She has also given talks on Alzheimer's to Tompkins Cortland Community College (TC3) nursing student classes and to Alzheimer-support groups at Walden Place in Cortland, NY and other locations around Central New York.

Additionally, Dafoe has given talks at the Cortland Rotary Club; the Rotary Breakfast Club in Homer; the Association of Writers and Writing Programs (AWP) annual, national conferences; and the New York State English Council Conferences.

Author and English educator **Nancy Dafoe** writes across genres and has had ten books published. In addition to *Naimah and Ajmal on Newton's Mountain,* Dafoe has written the Vena Goodwin murder mystery series which includes novels *You Enter a Room, Both End in Speculation,* and *Murder on Ponte Vecchio.* Dafoe's short stories and poems have been regionally and nationally recognized. Her poetry earned first place in the William Faulkner-William Wisdom creative writing competition (2016), and her short stories won first place and third place in the New Century Writer international competition. Other published books include her cross-genre memoir *An Iceberg in Paradise: A Passage through Alzheimer's,* a memoir about her mother's disease. She has also written textbooks on education and writing: *The Misdirection of Education Policy; Breaking Open the Box;* and *Writing Creatively.* She has a published book of poetry, *Innermost Sea,* and a chapbook, *Poets Diving in the Night,* through FLP. She is the Letters Chair for the National League of American Pen Women (NLAPW) and served as Central New York Branch President of the NLAPW. She writes monthly blogs on writing on her websites, nancydafoebooks.com and nancydafoefiction.com and offers professional development workshops. Her work appears in numerous journals and published anthologies, including *Lost Orchard* and *New York Votes for Women.* She lives in rural, Central New York with her husband Daniel.

CPSIA information can be obtained
at www.ICGtesting.com
Printed in the USA
FSHW010911080721
82926FS